T0118077

diary of a medium- stories of reincarnations

Andy A. Kay

iUniverse, Inc.
Bloomington

DIARY OF A MEDIUM- STORIES OF REINCARNATIONS

iUniverse books may be ordered through booksellers or by contacting:

iUniverse
1663 Liberty Drive
Bloomington, IN 47403
www.iuniverse.com
1-800-Authors (1-800-288-4677)

ISBN: 978-1-4401-9490-0 (sc)
ISBN: 978-1-4401-9491-7 (ebk)

Printed in the United States of America

iUniverse rev. date: 1/22/2013

Footprints of a traveler are the contents in the hymn
==== of the birds ====

Guest

Broken

Standard of a Fairy

Research

Quest

Fall

Silence on Fire

Recipe

The Latest Mode

Gold-Finger

Political Shoe

Countryside Hair Salon

A Little Touch

Karma of Tea

Extreme Offer

Against all odds

New Age Crap

Champ Shoe

Handmade Shoe

Two Left

Astrologist for One Day

The Guest

Walking along the street looking up at the high buildings in the city center, he nearly bumped into a woman exiting a shop. He paused beside its showcase window, which displayed a colorful array of shoes. After perusing them over for a while he entered the store and began picking up shoes off the racks, his fingers tracing, fumbling over laces and soles as if reading Braille script. Despite the suspicious glances that followed him, the customer tried them all, women's and men's shoes but none fit, and he left the store dazed and barefoot. The convincing words of the salesclerk that new shoes stretch over time were to no avail.

Down the street he found another shoe store, and tried on one pair after another.

"Are you from the green party?" the salesclerk asked him as he pressed the toe of one shoe. He looked up at her, surprised by the question, "No. I'm just a tourist."

Foreigners, she thought, noting the trail of scattered shoes he'd left behind him despite the end-of-season sale.

He stands in the middle of the city center; tries to get used to this new sensation of firm ground under his feet. He fell from the sky by mistake; his shriveled wings humped on his back, covered by a kind of jacket and wide pants he'd found discarded near a garbage can. With nothing on his feet though, each step is a concerted effort. He chooses his steps carefully, trying not to bump into passersby, all of whom have a kind of accessory that, when tapped on the sidewalk, makes weird echoes. They're obviously required.

He admitted he needed a pair. He planned to stay for a while; his wings were wounded, so it seemed he'd need to stay some time on earth. At least there seemed to be no problem getting these things called shoes. In a city with so many shoe stores as this, there must be a pair that fit somewhere.

When he asked in one store if they had shoes for angels though, the salesclerk just looked at him.

He didn't know what angels' shoes looked like or if they existed at all; he'd never needed any until now. He'd had no idea it would be so hard to find some shoes, even while moving so slowly. Nevertheless, he still failed to find any.

Walking on, he heard a kid passing by with his parents from the opposite direction whispering about him to his mother, "This man has no shoes."

The stranger, who heard him, explained that he was an angel.

"Have you lost your shoes during a flight?" the boy laughed as he walked away. "A clumsy angel."

Another shoe store, plenty of measuring work, and no results. His feet ached and at some point, he had to give them a rest. Sitting on a street corner, his back leaning against a wall, he looked at the crowded street. A birdsong emerged from somewhere among the tall buildings, then faded in the melee of cars and the orchestra of footsteps. A young woman shook her head in reply and stubbed out her cigarette before disappearing into a phone booth, one of several on the street corner. He looked down at the feet of those exiting the booths, one after another.

'The search must go on, while there is still strength left in my feet,' he thought a few minutes later. Rising again, walking on, he decided to cross the street. Ignoring the traffic, he lurched between cars, falling, rising again, horns honking on all sides. Somehow, he reached the sidewalk upright, proud. He asked passersby if they had nice shoes for him. Everyone just looked at him.

A pair thrown in the middle of the street caught his eyes. He approached, kneeled, and tried them on; the colorful sneakers were too big though, and slipped loose off his feet after a few steps.

It was a long day.

The city was not as big as it seemed to him but it was known for its beaches and the views around it - green terrains and small villages, which he was about to reveal soon.

He reached the suburbs. It was dark but he kept walking without realizing that he left the city striding through thick brush and tall grass. An hour later, a row of roofs tinged by the moonlight was revealed and he discovered that he was in a village that seemed deserted except for a shed with lightened windows. He hurried inside, sat at a table in the corner and stretched his aching feet out in front of him. It turned out to be the local bar. He was the only one in the room wearing a jacket. From his table by the window, his gaze drifted over the shoes of the customers; farmers and anglers in the middle of an end-of-a-work-day chat. After a while, a farmer asked the barefoot guest what brought him to the village, and he explained that he couldn't find shoes that would fit him anywhere. A face rose from behind the counter. The bar owner fumbled in the back and carried two worn boots. The long shoelaces were a complication but he grabbed them from her hands; something strange happened when he put them on his feet; he felt dizzy as if he entered into a thick gray cloud.

"What's wrong?" the bar owner asked him as he gave her back the boots.

"Too small; I'm looking for the kind of shoes that fit for a long journey," he finally said looking down at the shoes of the man next to him; the youngster was drinking from a glass of booze he was holding in his hand. "Can I check yours?"

The youngster looked at him but since the stranger was pleading to look more closely at the shoes, he took one off. The farmers watched the customer holding the boot in the air, as if measuring its weight. It was so heavy as if… there was something inside.

As he lay the boot on the windowsill, a breeze from the sea was playing with the shoelaces. He scooped the sleeves of his jacket, and as he fumbled it, he felt tinglings running down his arm. And suddenly, sights ran through his mind; shapes and forms came up as if from inside of the shoe. He wondered if the sights were from places the shoes might take him if he were to wear them.

Dazed, the stranger returned the boot to the young man; the latter saw nothing around him, but a dream he used to have entered into his memory, and as he wore the shoe, he felt it was more comfortable than before.

The customers opened a discussion about the dream, which wasn't over when the stranger left on his way.

Half a mile further, he entered another village to give his aching feet a rest. He found a noisy shed; a late party was going on. As he sat in the corner, people around him were dancing on the tables to loud music. Nobody noticed the fellow. He could be an angler — or perhaps a truck driver — munching on something at the end of a workday. Only the bar owner threw a glance at the stranger. He did not order anything. He just bent under his table, his gaze drifting over a few shoes when a dog trying to nap under a chair nearby growled at him; he sat up wondering what was in the shoes that made people so jumpy.

A young man in jeans and a flannel shirt seemed annoyed by his inquiring glances, and asked, "Can you explain why you are staring at me?"

"You have got nice shoes; they could be mine."

"No way! I bought them in the store a few months ago."

The barefoot guest explained that he was looking for angel's shoes, the only ones that might fit him.

"These are standard shoes; good enough for temporary jobs."

"What jobs?"

"All kinds of remounts and plumbing, dirty stuff that you need work boots for."

Considering it, the youngster took one boot off; maybe it was an angel's shoe. The suspicion on his face changed to surprise as the stranger laid it on the windowsill and said, "I see a lion."

"Recently I have been dreaming this dream," the youngster said. "I am home, sitting on the veranda drinking coffee. Suddenly, a lion comes from nowhere and jumps over me. We fight until I give him a piece of meat I had in the refrigerator just so the beast would leave. I wonder what this dream means."

"The lion must be part of you," the stranger said, "A symbol of your anger, pride and ego, which you cannot control. The king of animals will not tolerate an insult."

"I had a job last week, painting someone's house. I was very angry as I was paid only half of what had been agreed on," the youngster admitted. And as he wore his boot, he saw a lion dancing outside.

"Try to unleash your anger, face your fears. Everything is temporary," the stranger said. He was surprised by how many farmers, witnesses of the scenes, asked him to check their shoes hoping those were a kind of magic shoes.

One shoe after another, dream succeeded dream, opening up, many concerned with financial problems. Apparently, the local farms were on the verge of bankruptcy due to the tough competition of modern farms recently built in the area.

A few more shoes, and he walked away. He decided to stay in the countryside for a while. Every half a mile at least, he stopped for a rest in another village and to check on more shoes.

The rumors of a stranger searching for shoes spread among the villages. A wayfarer without shoes was an unacceptable sight in the countryside, and the customers in the bars often brought him worn pairs from their attics to try on. But he always found something wrong in their size or in his feeling when he wore them, so he dismissed them one by one. However, with each pair of shoes - sneakers, moccasins, slippers, he began to feel and see different things, shapes and forms that came up as if from inside of the shoe. The owner's dream, according to him, was stuck deep inside the shoe.

He traveled from one village to another, from one bar to the next. Entering a village, he said hello to the customers in the local bar, and asked for a shoe.

He had this special kind of ritual; he would lay the shoe on the windowsill and wait until the dream emerged outside as if from the shoe itself to his eyes only, complete with details which the shoe-owner had forgotten all about. Touching one's shoe, he tickled the soul and natural fountains of inspiration spring forth. He realized shoes projected the dreams in a different light – reflection of the owner's personality, which made them more sensible. The shoes provided a different perspective of a dream. Dreams were like a boat, leaving the bay of the soul.

He became a regular in the bars of the region, where dreams stalked waking thoughts. The bar owners were willing to save a table by the window for him. Some gave him a free meal and some a roof for the night. Everyone was secretly hoping that their shoes would turn out to be angel's shoes, developing all kind of theories about their powers.

Rubbing the toe of the shoe, he gave tips for advancing the owner's career or recommended buying new shoes. "Let the shoes lead. They know the way to arrange the best journey for the soul, fulfilling your dream, whether it is a big city, an evergreen forest, or a desert," he claimed.

Absurd itineraries were rather women's privileges and the food motif was popular. "Eat more solid food," he told one woman whose shoe imposed potato-shaped clouds drifting in the skies.

No one was surprised that his tips did not always give results and his prognosis of the future was often inaccurate. What can be expected from a man without shoes? One woman, who followed his advice to buy new shoes, complained that it didn't change a thing in her life. However, some found his advice more valuable than of the typical city psychic, whose advice was usually good for only one season a year.

There were many villages to explore. Every now and then, a rumor of a farmer, who found a pair of old shoes reached his ears, and the wayfarer would come to the farmer's village to check on them. He also used to ask the people he met on his way to check their own shoes closely. He tried even pairs in terrible condition thrown by the wayside.

Reading shoes was a tough job, no rest in it, but it must be done to find more shoes; one might fit him at the end.

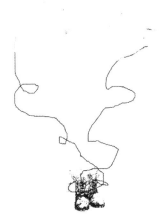

Broken Zone

On certain occasions, he shook the shoe to get a better view before laying it on the windowsill. Once, he shook the black shining shoe of the barman in one roadside dinner even longer, and the shoe featured a sailor sailing in the heart of the sea on an old boat that dated back to previous centuries. This opened a discussion about previous lives, whether a dream really happened or was it an ancient decision?

Few pairs of married couples in that dinner showed that their relationship started in a previous life, but in the opposite roles.

He also checked the shoes of one old man and a wide white screen unfolded. At first, he was not sure what it meant until voices sounded from within the shoe, "Tell the person he is sick, dying - he will join us soon; the end is near." The wayfarer dropped the shoe so the customer would not hear the spirits of the dead. Just before dropping it, he heard a muffled pounding from within, echoes of footsteps, which slowly faded.

He thought about it later while sitting in a bus station. Unexpectedly, a horse wagon arrived and since there was no bus in sight he decided to take a ride and climbed up.

He was sitting next to the driver, a pail-haired man, who whistled an old melody to the horse. They were heading to the southern edge of the countryside, where he found the climate warmer. The ride was pleasant, green terrains changing from both sides of the bumpy side road. From time to time, the driver shouted to the horse, who was moving fast on the winding route – no matter the eggs crates in the back of the wagon. The driver didn't seem to worry about it though.

"I must confess I have never met a vagabond without shoes," the driver, who was also barefoot, said.

"Good shoes are hard to find," the wayfarer explained. "And I haven't met a farmer without shoes."

"I feel a lot more comfortable like that, riding the whole day to sell these eggs anyway," said the farmer. "Eggs can break easily; they are as nearly sensitive as dreams. But this horse was a racing horse once, a true winner. No wonder he won all his races. He is not just running; he is floating on the road. A true winner must be sensitive to dreams and this horse must have had long dreams once, real adventures taking him to the other side of the world. I bought him after he retired."

They rode farther and faster passing by an old woman, who was walking at the side of the road with a goat. Further ahead, roofs tinged by red at sunset were revealed, roofs that seemed to be another village. Murmuring thanks, the wayfarer slipped down the wagon and said goodbye, noticing that not one egg was broken. However, his theory about it was different. "This horse is probably a reincarnation of a turtle. Whatever it carries gets home safely," he said, "since a turtle is the reincarnation of a spirit that carries a big secret from a previous life on its back."

The village was located on the border with another country, judging by the different jargons and accents he heard from people in the main street. He wished to start exploring for shoes, but questions rose by then: police officials picked up, "the investigator of the fairies", as they called the stranger, and took him to the nearby station for an inquiry. His reputation had spread far but he didn't know it had reached even there…

The chief observed the guy with the ruffled hair and the strange old-fashioned jacket. "Once I arrested a psychic from Africa, and he promised me I was going to be successful and rich if I let him go. I am still waiting," he murmured. The stranger just nodded wondering what the fuss was all about when he detected some energy coming from somewhere.

The chief and his cops followed him slowly through the corridors of the station; walking on he entered a room where stolen property, devices caught during the past year, were stored. The cops thought he might give them the names of the thieves or of the owners. Suddenly, a metallic creak cut through the room, and the cops looked at a CD player that rested on one of the shelves.

The chief turned toward one of the cops, "You said the device was broken, Carlson."

"It is, but a spirit is trying to contact us," the stranger interfered. His hand rose, swinging over the CD player as if he was cradling a baby. "Does anyone know a woman called Lilia?"

"Not I," said the cop called Carlson.

When another metallic rustle sounded, the chief coughed. "My grandma's name was Lola - she passed away a year ago."

The stranger turned toward the chief with wide-eyed indignation, saying in an utterly different tone of voice, "Shame on you - calling me through a stolen property. I refuse to speak with you until you behave."

"Tell her that the device is not mine," the chief murmured.

"I can't. The spirit has spoken - you hurt her. She saw it was stolen from a car earlier, and that is all that matters to her, not who stole it." The stranger picked up the CD player, and threw it. "Spirits do not see any difference - to them, stolen is broken."

The cops looked at the device crashed on the floor, playing chamber music.

After that, they took him to one crime scene where he knelt and saw colorful, glittering stains like dead leaves in the fall. These were footprints of dreams; each soul leaving unique footprints that shed the radiation of the dream on the ground. While some streets were clean, in others, there were plenty and they led to suspects. There was a case involving a shooting in the central bus station. By chance, there were no casualties, and no suspects. The police thought a drunken passenger quarreled with the bus driver. When the wayfarer arrived, he saw many footprints. The only witness was a bird perched on a roof nearby in a state of shock from the shooting; he picked a trail of footprints which led him to an old woman who was waiting for the bus.

With that, the police gave up on his service. After all, the old woman couldn't have been the shooter. Later, a security guard admitted that while he had been checking his weapon, he accidentally fired a bullet.

Once, a convicted bank robber asked to see the stranger. The man was wondering if the police suspected anything, as he was planning an operation. The stranger advised him to buy new shoes and free pigeons from a cage for luck.

Later, the robber broke into a pet shop in Suspicions Street and freed all the animals and the birds there, including a few pigeons that twittered gratefully while they flew away.

A dream is a rap song

on the top of destiny's chart.

The Startup of the Fairies

The storm whirled over the thick brush with no sign of stopping soon. A frantic tweeting could be heard through the rain and thunder, as a white parrot sought a hiding place from the terrible weather. The bird had been flying around for a long time, flying blindly while bumping into trees in its path. Nevertheless, with some kind of sixth sense, he reached a village and circled over a crooked chimney on one of the roofs for a minute, then flew smoothly inside through a window, the only open window. It was a bar, a shelter of comfort for many farmers waiting for the rough storm to pass. The place was as packed.

As the blind bird flew confused over their heads, the farmers wondered where it had come from.

"Whoever it lands on is going to be lucky today," one farmer decided, to boisterous laugher.

Another farmer suggested that the parrot might have been blinded after seeing an alien spaceship. He himself had met aliens, she claimed. They looked pretty human except for their scaly, lizard-like skin. They wore sort of pajama and had marked hatred for insects. The 'black box' of this spaceship was most probably very valuable. Many thought that eons ago these black boxes from alien spaceships had floated through outer space and that they had had a role in the evolution of humankind, serving as a kind of beehive of human souls.

The parrot landed at last and perched on the shoulder of an elegantly-dressed woman who was drinking tea at one of the tables.

"Mrs. Morgan is the lucky one," the farmers called.

"Go away," the woman sputtered angrily. The parrot seemed to feel quite comfortable on her shoulder though. He twittered in her ear letting out an imitation of a dog barking on the street outside. The farmers became enthusiastic over the parrot's abilities.

"You should treat him with more respect. Maybe this bird has recognized you from a previous life," said someone seated by the window.

The woman her colorful lipstick shining, turned to see the man who had commented. He had recently entered the pub and was dressed in a worn jacket and wide pants and was barefoot. Nevertheless, he seemed pleased by the stormy weather.

The fashionable and dignified woman explained to him that she did not believe in previous lives or souls. Nor was she a fan of extra-sensory perception and of alternate realities; never trusted palm-readers, fortune-tellers or crystal-peddling merchants who sold handmade jewels imported from Virginia as talismans. This fellow seemed to be one of that community. No so-called 'psychic' will teach *her* manners!

Mrs. Morgan was a member of the town's leading family and had studied at a famous university. She had found a job in a leading law firm in the state, where she had met her first husband. When they divorced, she decided to move to the countryside.

She turned to the farmers nearby as her witnesses as she said, "I trust only common sense these days."

"Common sense and logic are the murderers of destiny's justice," the stranger claimed.

"Yes, but that's got nothing to do with it. I just don't like psychics. When I was young, I met someone in a club. He was nice, I liked him, and we danced together. While we were dancing, he whispered things into my ear."

"What kind of things?"

"About the future." She raised the sleeve of her shirt to reveal a tattoo of a sleeping fairy near her elbow. "I even did this for him, but he never called back."

"You must have done the same thing to him in a previous life," the stranger offered.

"I don't remember any such thing."

"I'm here to remind you." He bent forward to look more closely at the tattoo. "Some souls are both so advanced and so vengeful that they wait a whole cycle to find the spirit that hurt them, to pay them back for the pain that they inflicted."

Mrs. Morgan was skeptical. The white parrot tossed his head from side to side and tweeted again with the same sound as heavy as a bark, as if in an answer to the whistling wind outside. He flapped his wings until a few feathers floated in the air like falling snowflakes. Suddenly she felt cold and sneezed. A shiver ran down her spine.

As she fondled him absently, the eyes of the pet half-opened for a second. Visions of snow flitted through her head and in her mind she saw snow-covered rooftops and a dog-shaped snow creature, walking an icy path and falling into a hole, swimming in icy water which reflected the stars.

"You are connecting to his dreams, to his dreams of the cold," the stranger informed her. "Animals' dreams can be rather delicate. Occasionally fairies get involved and help them, especially the blind ones. It's an investment for the fairies. It seems that a fairy helped you see the bird's dream because of the fairy tattoo on your elbow. It's a sign for them to appear."

"That makes no sense - what does the dream mean?" asked Mrs. Morgan.

"The reflections of the stars are reflections of a previous life, and promises of unexpected delights, such as finding a secret treasure hidden in the past, or receiving an inheritance."

"The bird has rich relatives?" one farmer laughed.

Mrs. Morgan shivered again as if a cold breeze from the sea had passed over her face. The parrot tweeted in her ear, and more visions flitted through her mind. White expanses, an apple-shaped palace up on a hill, dinner parties, sumptuous food; huge halls adorned with oil paintings, wild soldiers in shining armor, a king with a shaggy dog following him…

The stranger said knowingly, "The parrot could be a reincarnated spirit of this dog. He wants to go back to the palace."

"Why?"

"Out of habit and longing, probably. Something devastating happened in his previous life of a dog, and it opened a wound which he carries until now," the stranger explained."

"Are you really saying the bird is the reincarnated spirit of a dog?" a farmer who hadn't spoken until then asked. "I know an old castle about a hundred miles to the north," remarked another farmer. "A king lived there until he was exiled for corruption. His subjects accused him of hiding a treasure which has never been found. Maybe this king believed in reincarnation, which was common then, and he decided to put something aside for a rainy day. If the king had a dog that knew about it, the bird must be trying to hint at it."

The farmer nodded. "I don't believe in a previous life. But you know, I've heard of this computer program called Destiny Line. You upload a photo of your face, and DL turns it into a topographic scheme. The nose, cheeks, and eyes are like hills and valleys as seen from bird's eye vision. Then the program compares it to regions around the world, searching for the same topography as your face. This is supposed to be the place where you lived in a previous life circle."

As the discussion continued, Mrs. Morgan looked down to see the parrot sliding down to one of her shoes. Then he tickled the other shoe and flew back to her shoulder murmuring some words into her ears.

Death is a gentleman
A glowing tower of snow
Holes in the ice…

"How do I get rid of this bird?" Her voice trembled.

"There is nothing much to do, except maybe read poetry to him before you go to sleep. Pick a poem about summer. Poems are like a refreshing wind which can take the soul to a better place," the wayfarer explained. He was thoughtful looking at her shoes peeking out from under her table; they did not fit the woman's aristocratic aura. They were worn and tired-looking.

"Where did you find them?" he asked wondering what the reason for the parrot's arrival was.

"I noticed them by the side of the road when I was taking a walk around the village a few days ago, when the storm began," Mrs. Morgan explained. An interesting change from the many designer shoes in her collection. Maybe he was right, she thought. It was snowy in the north the entire year, which would explain her white visions.

On the next day, Mrs. Morgan set off to the castle. It was a long way by bus. Sitting on her shoulder, the parrot seemed unexcited, and if he knew where they were going, he didn't show it. The scenes she had been looking at through the window were replaced by her inner visions: wild soldiers dressed in shining armor, someone struggling in the snow carrying a sack on his back.

After journeying over a hundred miles to the north, the woman and her parrot reached the castle. It was located in a peaceful, snow-covered area. The castle had been turned into a museum and was the main attraction of the nearby small town. As soon as they entered the museum, the parrot swooped around the grand halls in excitement from one room to another, as if familiar with his surroundings.

*

Tension was in the air. Television crews, journalists, and ordinary citizens were standing on the stairway of the town's courthouse. A reporter shoved a microphone up to the bird that lay in Mrs. Morgan's arms, dressed in one of her fancy pullovers. "No comment," she snapped as she made her way to the door and entered into the hall. She hurried to take her seat.

"All rise!" someone called.

A woman in a long blue cap entered as the traditional princess of snow, and seated herself in a high chair, throwing a glance at a few reporters in the back of the crowded hall. She could not remember this courtroom has ever been so packed, except for the time years ago when one farmer blamed his neighbor for stealing beans. They all knew that Judge Muniz, called Ullu in the media, would not allow a circus in her courtroom.

She turned to her clerk, a man sitting next to her with his long bright hair drawn into a ponytail. "What is the charge?"

"Vandalism and inappropriate behavior in the national palace-museum, your honor."

Ullu gazed at the defendant. "What do you plead?"

"Not guilty," Mrs. Morgan stated.

"Do you have an attorney?"

"I will defend myself, as I am a trained lawyer, your honor," Mrs. Morgan said caressing the parrot on her shoulder. "Nobody denies the fact that the parrot caused damage, but since when it is illegal to damage your own property? We shall prove that as a close friend of the previous owner of the palace, he had the right to fly where he wished through the space. I want to point out that the mere sound of the word 'snow' causes the parrot to bark, shiver, sneeze and shake down to his very soul, as he remembers his king from the palace."

Ullu was puzzled. "Are you going to base your case on the claim that this cute little bird is the reincarnated spirit of a dog which lived in the palace?"

"How else would the bird know the exact spot of this package which the owner had hidden?" Mrs. Morgan retorted approaching the judge. She handed over a sack full of bills. These had been checked out earlier by an expert, who asserted that they were genuine and could be dated back centuries ago. "This is exhibit number one, your honor. Yesterday, after snooping around the castle, the bird found this behind a brick in one of the halls of the castle. One king had hidden this money long ago, while living here. Only his dog knew about it."

Ullu looked closely at the package when someone in the crowd cried, "Long live the king!"

A wave of whispers followed soon dying when Ullu picked her gable and knocked on her desk. "Silence in the court room!"

The prosecutor, a tall, bald man rose from his seat gesticulating toward a group of people sitting in the front row of the courtroom. "My clients, the descendants of the last king who ruled this country, are the legal inheritors of any money found in the castle."

The judge signaled him to proceed, and the prosecutor called his first witness, one of the museum's security guards, who described how he saw the parrot peeing in the corner of one room, scratching the wall; and how Mrs. Morgan was breaking a few bricks at that spot, pulling the package from there.

As the man slowly stepped down from the witness box, Mrs. Morgan strode forward, and another shout came from the crowd, "You're nothing but a common thief!"

A low rumble of whispers combined with the sharp tweet of the parrot. The judge raised her wooden gavel again and when silence fell she instructed the jury to ignore these comments. Mrs. Morgan called her first witness, the stranger from the pub, to testify as an expert in parapsychology. He seated himself in the witness chair. The white bird on his shoulder twittered a sort of muffled bark.

"Who is the witness?"

Mrs. Morgan replied, "*Both* are key witnesses, your honor."

"I'll allow it for now but I warn you - no monkey business," Ullu stated.

Patting the pet's head, the wayfarer swore to tell nothing but the truth, and began relating the dreams. "And the king's name was, "Clyde, Kale…Sky…""

He whispered a series of names into the bird's ear but no response came.

"Stop it," the judge tired of this farce. "This is ridiculous!"

The parrot suddenly barked rom the wayfarer's shoulder, "Long live the king!"

"Exactly!" the wayfarer said. "'Riddic' - that must have been the king's name." His testimony was finished.

As the chuckling reduced into silence, the busy clacking of the reporters' typing sounded from the back of the room.

The clerk interfered, "Perhaps he means King Rudi."

"Really? That's very interesting," the judge opined. "The king who ruled in this country eight hundred years ago?"

The clerk, who was more familiar with the country's history, replied, "Five hundred years ago, until he was found guilty of corruption and was exiled, your honor. Even his wife the queen could not help him then. He loved his dog very much though…"

The prosecutor coughed and began his cross-examination. "I was told that you can see angels. Are there any angels in the room at the moment?"

Mrs. Morgan stood up, "Objection, your honor. My colleague is provoking the witness."

The prosecutor replied, "I am trying to make a point about his qualifications."

"Overruled. Answer the question."

The wayfarer, with a vague gesture of his hand, his eyes passing over the room, answered, "There is no visible radiation of an angel at the moment. It is too cold for them, I suppose, but I sense other energies, probably fairies. They're crying, pleading, and I hear them saying, 'They're innocent; convicted by mistake.'"

Ullu asked, "What did you suppose they would say? They are always 'innocent'."

The prosecutor nodded, "I heard that you can also divine a person's previous life."

"Depends on one's shoes," the witness replied. He made a few more remarks about the rules of reincarnation, including the idea that souls choose their next life cycle, even the place of birth and the parents' social status. He compared it to buying shoes for a new trip.

The prosecutor turned toward the jury with a smile on his face. At that moment, the witness was telling Ullu about her previous life; he saw that in the parrot's dreams, which meant they knew each other back then. Her gavel remained hanging in the air. Silence reigned in the hall.

The wayfarer also mentioned that lawyers were the reincarnated spirits of criminals.

The prosecutor annoyed, whispered with his clients, King Rudi's descendants, who complained that the parrot was staring at them. Then he turned toward the judge, "We demand full punishment for the defendants. This courtroom should follow the law, not dreams. Nothing stands above the law. Everything else is speculation."

It was a long trial…

The reporters wrote, "The question in front of this courtroom today is whether this parrot is the reincarnated spirit of the dog of king Rudi, who wrote his name in the pages of this country's history as the most beloved king ever, until his exile…"

*

Mrs. Morgan was rather surprised when she won the trial. But judge Ullu turned out to be a person who believed strongly in reincarnation, even fancying herself as the reincarnated spirit of Rudi's wife, Queen Evelyn, as the wayfarer declared. This obviously affected the verdict.

Before letting the defendants go, however, Ullu decided to put them to a test. In the back of the castle, there was a labyrinth, which King Rudi had built. Therefore, Ullu said that if the bird was truly the king's dog, he should know the way out.

The woman and her parrot were taken into a small cell in the castle's dungeon basement, which was the center of the labyrinth. Mrs. Morgan started searching for a way out but the parrot flew against a large oil painting hung on the wall, as if he actually saw it. The picture seemed as if it had been there for hundreds of years. She tried to observe it more closely, but it was too dark to see the figures. The parrot, however, barked loudly scratching frantically at the canvas. At first she thought he needed to pee, but when he kept barking for attention, she removed the painting from the wall, and there she saw the entrance to a tunnel. The parrot rushed forward and she followed, crawling on her knees in the dark. Echoes of barks led the way toward a light, and a vision of colorful feathers on the other side of the tunnel. A few moments later, they were standing outside the castle walls. People who had followed the defendants from the courtroom and waited nearby were joined by some of the distinguished citizens of the town, political, social and religious leaders. They all began cheering, since their escape was a proof of their innocence.

The bird looked dazed, gliding like a snowball toward the crowd, and fell straight into Ullu's arms.

"Welcome back," the judge said, proud of the justice that her courtroom had dealt out. "At last we meet again. You are acquitted, free to go now. You are 'a king witness', if I may say so."

His eyes suddenly opened. He was blinking from the blinding white expanses of snow; he could see! He was healed!

On the morning after her return, Mrs. Morgan told the farmers in the bar that she had won the case but the old bills were unfortunately of no monetary value, only historical interest. "We left the money to the museum. Rudi should have hidden diamonds back then, not bills. Right, Maxi boy?"

"The name of King Rudi's dog was Max," Mrs. Morgan explained fondling the pet who lay in her arms, proudly leaking an apple pudding from a plate that lay on her table. His eyes were twinkling with pleasure.

Everyone in the bar clapped but the farmers refused to believe the parrot's eyes were healed, until he jumped to the floor, and stood for a moment against an oil painting hung on the wall, barking as if seeing details no one else did. It was the same picture that had hidden the tunnel in the castle, a souvenir given to them by the museum. The picture was a portrait of three figures: the royal couple, King Rudi and Queen Evelyn, dressed in their fancy clothes and a small shaggy dog that lay between them eating an apple.

The wayfarer observed Queen Evelyn's shoes. They resembled the ones that Mrs. Morgan was wearing, only shiny and new. She had dreams of the cold the next days, and when she informed the wayfarer about it, he asked to see her shoes. As he shook them, two snowballs fell out, one from each shoe. He tried the shoes on, but of course they didn't fit him.

Even so, he said the spell of the shoes was gone and that the dreams would not bother her or the parrot anymore. From this day forward, she would sleep peacefully.

"The parrot expects his owner, the king to come back now that he is acquitted," the wayfarer claimed.

As he left on his way, Mrs. Morgan wore the shoes, strolling around the room and trying not to slip on the melted snow on her way to the door. The parrot joined her in a walk around the village. The storm passed and the bird flew around happily ever after, although now and then he would bump into trees. Sometimes Max the bird perched on Mrs. Morgan's shoulder staring at the portrait. Then he would fly away, grabbing an apple from a plate on one of the tables. The farmers tried to make him imitate people, as a normal parrot would, but the parrot would have none of it, flapping with his wings, barking whenever a street dog barked outside.

One day, a farmer from the village decided he wanted a dog. He bought a furry, small one, and he took the dog for a walk around the village; it barked at the exotic bird that perched on the bar's roof; Max stared at the dog; he seemed stunned and ashamed.

"Rudi...is that you?" the parrot barked aloud plaintively, chasing the dog, which ran away, frightened, despite the farmer's attempt to hold him. "I'm sorry I took the treasure, Rudi; but, you took *my* body, didn't you? Long live! Long live the king!"

> *In the court room of souls, fairies are the jury, and a dream is the verdict.*

A dream is the verdict

*

Only after the wayfarer had left, did some old farmer remember that he heard people mentioning an odd man walking around lately, searching for shoes that would fit him. He had become a regular subject of gossip in the bars of the region. They spoke of the fellow who always wore the same worn clothes and walked barefoot. The farmer had even heard that this person had tried on so many shoes that he had developed all kinds of extra-sensory abilities. People came from the big city asking for his advice.

Some said he simply had a fetish for shoes and that his dream-interpreting was just an excuse to touch as many shoes as possible.

He spent some more time in the countryside reading shoes, reciting interpretations. It was not clear if it was really that no shoe fit him, or if he was searching for a particular pair of shoes - angels' shoes. Different rumors spread about their qualities. People who found some old shoes by the wayside wondered if those were the ones which do miracles.

Sometimes, in rough areas, he put on a pair of shoes which were too tight, and walked with them for a while, but after a mile or two he threw them away before entering the bar of another village. The mayor of that village offered to appoint him as a social worker, as solving dreams was a full-time job and a necessary service to the community. But the barefoot stranger kept going; he still seemed to be waiting for a pair of shoes, which fit him. There were many villages to visit. Moments were woven in grief as his feet ached so much on his way. More than once, he fell all over on the ground but he was not ready to give up yet, rising again.

One day he disappeared. Some claimed he returned home; others said that he tired of the dream-solving business and he went to the big city, to check on fancy shoe stores in there.

Some dreams are a repetition of the future.

Quest

It was March, and the small park - a shelter of peacefulness and grace from the whirl of modern life in the city center, was cold and sunny. He was used to passing his lunch breaks in his warm office in one of the country's largest travel agencies - it occupies a whole top floor of the high-riser. But today, as he stood for a moment by the window looking out, he wished to go outside; to sit on one of the benches at the park across the street; they were placed in a circle under a stand of trees.

He sat with a plastic cup of coffee in his hand, with the wind blowing about him, bringing a leaf which landed over him, among other colorful leaves, as an old memory of the rainbow. Watching the cars passing on the crowded boulevard stretching next to the park, he was not paying attention to the person sitting on the other end of the bench. While his gaze drifted over to the building he had just left, his neighbor asked what was so interesting in the building.

"I work there," the man replied, and turned his gaze to see who had addressed him. The guy was dressed in a worn jacket and wide pants. To complete the picture, he was barefoot, despite the cold weather.

"Is it hard work?"

The travel agent coughed; thinking about it, he remembered an old couple who were interested in the Pacific Ocean Cruise earlier that morning. "You must to know all kinds of touring possibilities, as making and cancelling reservations, all that sort of thing."

The guy nodded. "I could work there myself."

"I don't think we're hiring any new agents at the moment," the travel agent said. "Do you have any experience?"

"You could say so. I am deeply familiar with the travel industry," the guy said. "I have a special vision about it."

"And what is that?"

"Shoes define the dimensions and destination of a journey. Let me see one of your shoes and I'll show you."

The travel agent looked at him, shrugged, and took off one of his shoes.

It was an elegant, classically-styled shoe. The stranger picked it up and held it in the air, as if measuring its weight. "I'd say you've owned these shoes for about a year," he said, his fingers running all over the shoe from the laces to the toe. "You are going to travel soon."

"Where to?"

"I can't see any specific place," said the guy as he swung his arms oddly.

The travel agent was silent. He really couldn't afford a trip anyway these days. He was fumbling his pockets for a cigarette, but he had none left. "I try to quit smoking, since my company doesn't permit it. But it's hard," he said.

"It *is* hard. But I know of a healer who has been working in the nearby towns. He helped many people to quit. They couldn't put a cigarette in their mouth anymore, and I'm talking about heavy smokers with yellow teeth. This healer is me…

"The sole is the soul of the shoe;" the stranger fondled the shoe's sole, played with the shoelaces, and held the agent's shoe over his head, "Smoking stems from guilt over things done in previous life cycles, and lighting a cigarette is an unconscious way of trying to 'burn' old sins. A self-superior approach is the gravitation of the soul. From this day forwards, each time you fancy a cigarette, your shoe will become hot and you will have to run."

"That's it?" the travel agent asked when the guy returned the shoe to him. Wearing it, he felt nothing special.

His neighbor nodded. "I would like to travel around the world myself one day."

The travel agent searched his pockets again, drawing out some brochures. "We offer all kind of tours."

But the odd person did not seem interested. "I need to find good shoes first."

"I can recommend a few stores for travelers with quality shoes," the travel agent said.

"I have been to many shoe stores in the city but I can't find a pair of shoes that fit correctly. It's not easy." The guy bent forward, and scratched his foot. "Nothing is more important than comfortable shoes; nothing more refreshing than putting on good shoes in the morning…I have even searched in the countryside. I thought there might be a better chance to find shoes in some village, rather than in the big city."

"Isn't it risky?"

"It's risky not to take risks," he smiled.

He added that he could not walk in shoes that didn't fit, although sometimes, on a rough route, there was no other choice but to put on a pair that was too big or too tight and then throw it away after a mile or two. He called those pairs a temporary comfort. "I was walking along a river once. Gold seekers were standing in the water, their boots thrown on the ground nearby. I stole one pair and they were so tight I threw them away after half a mile."

The guy paused, swinging slightly on the bench; he had a weary look in his eyes. "I don't understand how I haven't found anything yet after searching in every village in a radius of few miles."

Suddenly he rose and said that he had to resume his search, edging his way toward the crowded boulevard across the park with no further explanations. A few teenagers threw sideway glances at him as the guy passed near their bench. He bumped into a woman walking from the opposite direction and the shopping bag she carried was smashed between their bodies. Groceries spilled all over. He looked down escaping her angry glance, but her shoes did not seem to be the kind that would fit him and so, he walked away.

The travel agent followed him with his gaze until his figure disappeared in the crowded boulevard.

Another leaf landed over him; it floated eloquently, as a member of a workaholic troupe of nature; a sign it was time to go. His lunch break was over. Up on his feet, he was striding toward his office. He met all kinds of people at his work in the agency but the odd pretentious guy from the park was far from the typical tourist.

*

He woke up early the next day. Although he had a car, he decided to take the bus to work that morning, a half hour's trip from the suburb where he lived.

Another ordinary working day in the office – long discussions with clients about their organized tours and flights began.

On his lunch break, he did some errands and when he was done, he went to the park and sat on the bench, the one he was on the other day. His eyes were focused on a fancy car when he noticed the same stranger coming from the street. He was dressed as he had been the day before, as if he had been shopping in a second-hand store. And still barefoot. The guy noticed him and approached, soon slumped down with a sigh on the other end of the bench.

"Still haven't found anything?"

"Not those I need," the wayfarer-looking person murmured and eased backward, his mud-flecked bare feet stretched forward. "My feet ache for shoes. Just this morning, I took a trip to visit another village by the sea, checking shoes, as many as possible, with no results… But I had a dream the other night."

"What was it about?" the travel agent raised his voice, making himself heard over the roar of cars from the nearby street.

The answer wasn't surprising .

"There was a tower made of shoes, one on top of the other stretching high up in the sky and then swallowed by clouds in a footprint shape. As if all the shoes I have tried on until now became a sort of ladder. I was going to climb up but then the ladder fell apart and the shoes became birds flying away; their twits sounded long after. The birds did not just sing a song, but told me something. I couldn't understand though."

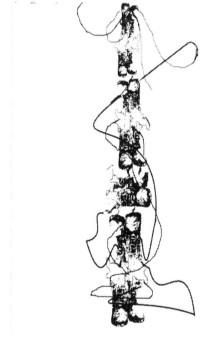

A pause and, "Anyway, checking shoes of all kinds, new and used ones, I have learnt what determines the path one takes and the place one goes to. Shoes are an authentic connection between the traveler's soul and the ground. Shoes are the missing link."

"Link to what?"

"To the future. I have tried so many shoes that when I touch a shoe, I see the views it offers, the places I might go to if I were to wear them, and I can decide to go there or not," the guy explained. "Inside some used pairs I've checked, I've found tiny stones. In others, I've found a piece of wood, plastic, and even a bit of sand. I've also seen plants and flowers growing from inside some shoes. I've met people who have found the same piece of material in their shoes every morning, over and over again, until their dream was solved."

"What are you saying?"

"Shoes bare one's dreams. The stones are dreams that become stuck in shoes. They get out after the dream has been solved, by shaking and swinging the shoe. Then they fall loose, dreams materialized."

The wayfarer felt the following silence from his neighbor on the bench, who was obviously trying to fathom his words.

His eyes drifted over the park; suddenly, he rose and went to one of the other benches. Underneath the bench was a pair of shoes. The travel agent followed him with his gaze. He presumed they belonged to a homeless person who had slept there the past night.

The wayfarer hurried, as if he were afraid that somebody else might take them. He returned to his acquaintance and waved two artificial leather shoes. He fumbled one shoe for a moment and then passed to the other shoe, one with a hole in the sole. "A strong dream made that hole," he announced and shook his head while fondling the shoe's sole. "It's probably about changing a career… The person who had left these shoes was probably a farmer from a far-away village who wanted a change."

The travel agent looked at him, puzzled.

"I saw a goat standing on the road trying to catch a ride but there were only hats floating in the wind. One hat fell on the ground, and the goat ate it. Road trips imply drastic decisions," The guy explained. "The owner of these shoes could also have been a goat in a previous life."

He tried the shoe on, but it did not fit his foot and he gave up. He returned them both to the place he had found them.

"These shoes might fit somebody else," the guy said; and when he sat back on the bench, there was a somewhat longing gaze in his eyes. "Everyone dreams, even if they cannot remember it the next morning."

"I don't." The travel agent shrugged unconvinced, pulled his hand out of his pocket and looked at his watch.

The guy was somewhat angered by the travel agent's indifference. "You must see the bird; there is one in every dream; seeing it, you remember the dream. Yesterday, I did see something in your shoe though."

"Did you?" The travel agent said, and took off one of his elegant shoes with no hesitations this time.

"I'm sure I'll find some forgotten dream."

Arms swinging…running fingers…

"It is a bit vague - two eyes," the wayfarer informed. "Almond-shaped eyes, unusually large, like leaves, brought by the wind, to this park…"

"It doesn't say much to me."

"I confess, it's not clear to me either," the stranger murmured. "It could be part of your future. Your destiny waits here, in the park."

The guy returned the shoe to him, and when he wore it, the travel agent thought it was just a coincidence that the mere thought of a cigarette made him sick.

"Everyone needs shoes that fit. Me, I haven't found the right ones yet." The guy scratched his foot again. "During the search in the countryside I have heard all kinds of rumors of shoes; some might have fallen from the sky. Have I mentioned that legend about shoes of angels?"

"Real angel's shoes…?" The agent was stunned.

The guy nodded. "Real shoes… The legend says that such shoes can take you to places never seen before. Me, if the shoes fit me, that's enough. I just want to travel around the world a bit. You haven't found some nice old shoes lately, haven't you?"

The agent was from a small town far from the big city. He had arrived two years before and stayed after finding the job in the travel agency. With all of his experience as a travel agent though, he had never encountered such passion for shoes. *The last person I would suspect to be an angel,* he thought while listening to the guy sharing his memories of his research that started since the day of his arrival to town.

Trees stretch their hands to see their leaf-shaped watches.

Dreams are ingredients in the recipes of destiny.

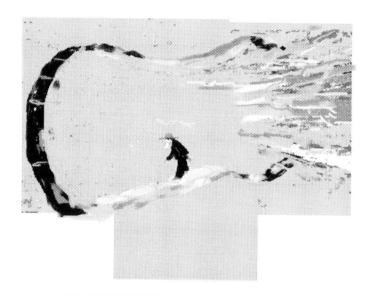

*A dream is a rainbow at night,
flushed out by the colors of
eternity.*

Research

He was circling in the sky in the role of the screen saver of earth, as every angel does, making no plans to pay a visit below, never even thought about it. Never missed the sense of time and place. For no particular reason, he felt great that day. Until soon, he found himself in a maze of indefinable clouds. He felt himself drowning in the gray, unfamiliar smells and noises from all over; he followed an odd sensation under his feet; a firm ground. So called earth...

He lurches among cars, falling, rising again, horns honking on all sides; each step a tough mission. Somehow, he reaches the sidewalk, upraised, proud. He stands still in the middle of the town center, his shriveled wings humped on his back, uncannily similar to clothes some passersby wore: a kind of jacket and pants. With nothing on his feet though.

At first, getting these things called shoes seemed easy with so many shoe stores in the street. He paused beside one showcase window looking over shoes for sale. His jacket changed color slightly, as he entered and tried some on, soon leaving disappointed.

Another shoe store, plenty of measuring work, no results. The pressure on his feet grew constantly; but the further he walked, the stronger the drive to travel by foot overtook him; to play his heart. He started all over, philandering through another neighborhood where he joined two homeless folks riffling through a garbage bin. There was nothing interesting inside; only an alley cat sprang from within and raced off as it if trying to rid itself of devils riding on its back.

A pile of shoes thrown nearby caught his eye; pairs and singles lay promisingly. But as he picked and touched one worn out with his hand, and tried on the shoe, he noticed that the space around him was changing, hung heavy. It was not his size. He threw it away, his hand fumbling, picking out another shoe from the pile, a silver-rose one that ran different views through his mind like a shockwave; views that seemed to come from places the shoe would take him to if he were to wear it. Then he heard a muffled pounding from within, echoes of footsteps, which grew into a voice. "I want to reincarnate," it said, fading, rising again. "Solve my dream…it is stuck inside the shoe…"

In a reflex, he threw the shoe into the garbage bin. Although it belonged to a dead person, the shoe seemed still alive.

He kept walking in the dark passing through the suburbs, one after the other. The shoes of passersby varied hugely the farther he walked. Soon he was out of the city; a few crooked roofs were revealed in the moonlight… He discovered that he was in a village.

*

No one knew when it had begun, but many bar owners claimed that the fellow who came from nowhere solved his first dream at their place. In a short time, his reputation spread as wide and fast as did jokes about his ritual, laying shoes on the window invitingly, whispering about, and fumbling as sort of a hacker. Entering a bar, he asked for a shoe. First, the customers just looked at him, but after visiting several villages, his reputation went ahead of him as a master of the shoe-reading technique and he had no problem checking any shoe he fancied; one might fit him at the end. With morning, he entered into a new bar and opened the window, fumbling shoes like a gardener checking the flowers in the morning to see what sprouted overnight and what is about to bloom. Vague dreams flit clearly in transparent views of a 360 degrees panorama to his eyes only, and he could walk straight toward solutions. He tried to wear some, enjoying their views; none fit, but shoes interpreted the owner's dreams.

Each shoe he laid on the windowsill unfolded a beauty before him. He improved his technique, revealing that touching the sole unfolded the biography of the soul, things forgotten all about, and shoelaces unfolded the future. It made him realize that shoes choose a road for the traveler by conducting an authentic connection between the soul of the shoe's owner and the ground.

"Other shoes lead to better places and other results," he claimed. "Any illness is a result of an unsolved dream; the symptom of the soul leads to the cure of the body."

After solving a dream and returning the shoe to the owner, something often fell out from within; a piece of stone, wood and even plastic. They said it was nothing important but he decided that those things were flushed out from the shoes as a result of the dream.

His efforts to find fit shoes continued but it was not going anywhere. He did not stay for long in one village but soon after his departure, local kids devoted their entire after school hours either for mind reading or for fore sighting and moving objects with their minds although he did not do any of those things. In one village, the locals even claimed that dogs' barks were foretelling the future.

When night fogged away quickly, the sun rose surprised, sending solved dreams, light beams through the window of another bar. Entering, groping his way, the wayfarer bumped into a chair until he found a free seat and stretched his aching feet forward looking out of the window. It was rainy and a rainbow stretched across the sky.

He heard two women sitting on the bar gossip. One woman sent sideway-glances while talking with the bar owner. "Go to speak with him before customers come over. He sees medical problems and says what vitamins one needs. Some of his studies are not accurate lately but there is nothing to lose."

She was more familiar with the reputation of the countryside phenomenon. "Some of his studies are not coherent but there is nothing to lose… Businessmen are his biggest fans. I think he just acts as a psychologist for them."

The other just nodded being the typical type of bar owner that never seeks advice from psychics and healers. "Marsha, The world has become a motel for superstitions; there are always free rooms…My sister believes in the stars. When she was engaged, she consulted an astrologist. Hearing the diagnosis about her fiancée, she cancelled the wedding and later married the astrologist. Everyone needs to believe in something. Some people carry mascots. Some just want tips and taps on the shoulder. For others, herbs imported from Virginia are more precious than jewels. Some can tell you things by looking at palms, drained coffee cups, or magic beans; and this guy reads shoes."

The bar owner went to the kitchen to fulfill her duties then was remorseful, bringing to the wayfarer the soup of the day, and a shoe - the shoe of the day.

He invited her to his table but she said that her back ached and she could not sit down. Of course, she didn't remember her dreams. Her friend threw a doubtful glance from the bar shaking her head.

"Dreams are the code of the universe; gifts from the soul. Cherish them!" he chided on her. Laying the shoe on the windowsill, he was fascinated by the knocking of the sharp high heel shoe on the wooden windowsill. It came in the quality of a sound effect beyond nature in his inexperienced ears.

His hand was sliding backward and forth over the white leather until she sighed, "Stop."

"Why?" he asked.

"Because it feels as if you are touching my back. It aches. Slowly."

His fingers moved again; finger after finger dancing to the rhythm of the raindrops knocking on the window. Then, he strongly pulled the shoelaces and the woman sighed and her back suddenly curved, as a sharp wave of pain passed through her body; it wasn't as tender as the touch but she felt like new as if a beam of light fell over her face. She remembered her dream. "I saw a pigeon tries to get out of my room through a narrow crack in the wall. It failed again and again. Finally, I opened up a window and the bird flew away. When I looked outside, the bird was a small spot in the distance."

He nodded. "I want to hear your opinion first. What would you make of that?"

The bar owner frowned. "A pigeon is the symbol of peace, isn't it? It's probably about my cousin; he is a soldier fighting in the war and I pray that he would come home safe."

The wayfarer shook his head, his hand rising over the shoe. "Leave the world peace for others. The bird stands for a part of your personality that is stuck. You open a window for yourself. Follow your dream. You become restless otherwise, like the pigeon. 'Opening the window' means you need a change in your real life, changing career or simply your address… in order to meet a nice fellow. Your wish will come true; soon, you would meet someone; someone who cares about birds as much as you do; he might be the one for you."

She went to the kitchen and when she returned the wayfarer wasn't there.

Later, when all the other customers left, she was sitting all alone with her thoughts at one table by the window. After work, she used to hang around with her friends but that afternoon they set her up with a blind date. She thought the person got scared. That moment, the door opened and a big charming dog entered and sat down at her table.

"What's your name?" she tried to open a conversation but he was just staring at her silently.

"Do you want something to eat? How old are you?" she tried again. He growled restlessly and his eyes rolled as if he was bewildered. Suddenly it stood up on its feet ready to attack. Her breath stopped as it lunged forward floating by her toward the open window landing outside. A flitting bird was seemingly his target.

"What has got into you, running after birds? Are you a baby?" She uttered. Rising from her chair, she could still hear barks and whistles further down the street.

"A dog is not simply following a dream, but running after it," she concluded deciding to avoid any blind dates in the future.

> *A dream is the tattoo of the soul.*

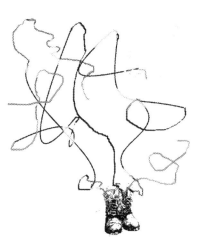

Silence on Fire

An unexpected meeting in one bar changed the direction of the research.

Days passed by in the countryside. He was walking with a cane, and with a tight pair that he had found at the side of the rough road. He threw the shoes after a mile before he entered another village; slumped down on a chair, as much lost as a sailor in the sea of expectations, he studied the shapes and sizes of some of the shoes peeping under one of the tables, three pairs in the three basic colors. They belonged to three jostling housewives. One of them, with a paled nose coughed disapprovingly, mentioning he could stay in this bar under one condition, if he reads something in a poetry reading engaged later on that evening.

The woman picked out of her pocket a sheet of paper and handed it over along with a pen.

"What should I write about?" The wayfarer took a sip from his coffee when the second housewife her eyes closed, said, "Listen... Do you hear it? Wings flutter. Angels fly somewhere! You just have to listen as the flutter becomes words far away in space."

The third kissed him on the cheek and his ruffled beard twitched as if in a search for a poem long after.

The first housewife rose from her chair walking toward the podium in the corner of the room with a notebook clutched in her hand. "The flutter… I hear it louder now… Two are flying out there on their way here."

Farmers giggled as she started reading.

> *Where has the rainbow gone?*
> *Has anybody seen, anybody heard?*
> *Colors lost one by one,*
> *One color here, one color there,*
> *Another rises in Monaco,*
> *Grown pale again*
> *I wish you'd tell me,*
> *Just show me the right way…*

When she made her dramatic pause taking a glass of water, a worried, puzzled face of a bartender rose from behind the counter. "Close the windows. Angels always leave a mess."

It was too late. A white light broke through one of the windows. No one expected this but a delirious long wing angel was revealed. Then, another one and third followed… Two creatures sprang into the room wing to wing, hovering from one shoulder to the next flapping over the customers. The rhythmical flips sounded like the swish of a washing machine. One angel stretched a long hilarious wing to fondle a cat which escaped under a table in the corner.

The bar owner prepared her specialty, his favorite cocktail called 'L'ev', made of corn, rose oil, and honey - a drink for 'a better flight', so the angel claimed. "I can teach you to fly…If witches fly, everyone can. Writing and reading a poem, as flying, require fitting into the right rhythm. You have to feel the beat as a drummer in the band of the universe, neither fast, nor laid-back. 'In the pocket'. Conformation and coordination are at the essence here…"

He was demonstrating, and few farmers waved with cowboy hats and casks in the air following the motions of his wings. A feather was floating in the room as if trying to avoid the observant eyes of the cat.

Circling, the other angel passed by the wayfarer and sat down at his table, asking, "Have I seen you somewhere before?"

The wayfarer hesitated before telling about his earthy research but the angel rose anxious to share a poem, a few lines he wrote during his flight down to earth.

Everybody became silent as he climbed up onto the stage reciting, his outstretched wing revealing a tattoo which read '*Keep off*'. The bartender closed her eyes, as if sailing away on a boat...

> *This raindrop is not mine,*
> *It is the sweat of a flying angel*
> *Falling…*

The wooden podium creaked under the angel's feet as if it was about to crack any moment; while the words flowed in the room, the angel flipped his wings passionately as if one wing didn't know what the other was doing. He slowly lifted into the air unaware that until his wings hit the ceiling. He lost his balance and tumbled on the floor. Rising again, he flew away through the window, followed by his fellow angel. After they disappeared into their wings, a moment of silence passed in the room. It all happened so fast that the wayfarer didn't have a chance to ask them anything.

"Look what they have done," the bartender said sorrowfully, dreadfully looking at the few mugs that lay crashed on the floor. The angels had hit everything in a wide radius around them while flying around the room.

After cleaning the mess, she went back on her accounts.

"Angels come and go," the second housewife her eyes still closed, uttered. "I have met them before. Every angel has his ups and downs."

The wayfarer looked at her. "Do you know where I can get shoes of angels?"

"Real angel's shoes…?" she said, "I heard a few people mentioning an extraordinary pair they found at the side of the road. There is a legend that an angel lost it when they fell off his feet. When someone puts them on the windowsill in his bedroom, one next to other, his dream comes into existence by morning; when he wakes up and looks outside, he sees a new path, so, he can walk on it later. He can travel with the shoes, explore a new landscape."

The wayfarer was silent.

A minute later, the housewives sang in chorus:

Words fly to their separate ways,
As the moment disappears,
Light is strong, peaceful
And darkness is a string
Of clouds,
Stretched all the way behind a smile of dawn,
And below,
A wave turns in bed of lost chances,
And the wind blows and whistles,
She sings a song about everything
She brings forgotten smells and words
And some flowers,
She is the guide of an old newspaper
A trip into the street corner's opened arms
Then she goes silent and alert,
Maybe she lost her way
In this gray street,
Lost together with memories and moments
A tear of heaven on the horizon in this moment,

This moment is a tear of heaven's fear.
Silence on fire,
The future is the last edition of us all...

The wayfarer decided it was time to go before the end of the poem.

Outside of the bar, he met the long winged angels passing the corner preparing for the flight back to heaven.

"It's not easy to stay down here especially with wings on your back. It is not recommended to stay on earth more than a few hours on earth anyway," the two said when he refused their offer to join. They gave him a few wing taps and tips. Nothing refreshed his memory though; and there was no sign that his allegeable wounded wings were recovering.

But the wish to travel overtook him and he asked them if they knew how to get angels' shoes. They looked at each other and one of them, who called himself Boy, claimed that angels were not supposed to travel around the world by foot as shoes that fit them did not exist. Only in ancient times, so some say, there was a type of shoes made especially for angels so they could use it on earth, but they were no longer available, not anymore, lost. What is lost is lost. Those were heaven's rules. Even old, high ranked angels could not recall how they looked except that they were shoes and were necessary, highly recommended equipment on earth. There were rumors of one pair found recently...an angel lost it while flying. But he could not count on it, unless... He might be the one who had lost it.

He couldn't remember such thing as the fall made his memories of the past too vague in his head. If he finds those shoes though, wearing them, so they said, his memory might return and his wings would function normally. Angels' shoes could be the kind of passport he needed to return to his world…

He watched them flying and when their wings were tangled on the horizon, he was out of the poets' village. Could he trust those rumors? Was there a point staying around? He might be searching for something that did not exist. But, he still had powers left before having to fly back to heaven. A wayfarer does not give up so easily. Especially when a footprint-shaped cloud hanging above was giving him hope.

Walking slowly, he aimed toward the shining tall buildings that cropped up ahead in the distance. After all this time, he decided that he should try to find fit shoes in the city once more.

Through the countryside's green terrain, past one village on his way, he heard twits of some kind of bird, which made him turn his head to the roof of the local post office. He never understood why the post offices were big buildings even in small villages; but it was a good place for the bird to rest perched on the roof tossing its head, whistling a nice melody.

He stood still. Birds never sang like that in the places he had come from. The whistles sounded utterly different when the bird flew away, and he wondered what was inspiring it, noticing its small shadow fluttering rapidly as a telegram on the ground farther and farther until it was lost from sight… A melancholic, peaceful melody of twits sounded in his ears almost as a coded message long after…leading the way… He was more that curious to know where it was flying. Was the whistling wind inspiring it?

Back in the city, to a familiar noisy rush, he walked around in one of the suburbs. Everything seemed the same as in the day of his arrival. He entered through a gleaming door. The chances of finding fine shoes were minimal in a tri-level mall though. The imperious glances of saleswomen followed him, two or three at each shoe store, a few per mall level. Finding nothing useful there, he left as much relieved as exhausted.

Soon, he vanished on a road sprawling for miles of peddlers and merchandise, goods of all kinds dotted about within the stalls. Mingling around, he was impressed by a tiny tool on one of the stalls that easily sucked the juice out of a lemon. In the whole flea market though, he found only one kind of shoe in a small size, the typical type made in the Far East, and they were uncomfortable.

On the way into the city center, he rested in bus stations since they seemed a popular spot to dispose of unnecessary clothes. There were used or new clothes thrown in many stations as well as shoes. Seated in one crowded station, he tried a lovely pair found there. While he tucked his foot inside, messing with the shoelaces, a car driving nearby suddenly turned straight toward the station. He moved but with the shoe still on, he was losing orientation, shaking his leg to get rid of the shoe until it fell loose. This pair clearly wasn't for him.

He approached a parked cab.

The driver glanced in the rear-view mirror at the stranger slumped in the back. "Have you got any money?"

"No, but I can read your shoe."

The driver nodded; his mustache twitched knowingly a moment later, when the wayfarer returned the shoe to him along with a few healthy tips.

"Where to?"

"Anywhere. Drive around in circles. This city is bigger than I thought."

As the car rolled off, the wayfarer gaped out the window.

"You looking for something in particular?" The driver asked.

"Shoes; I lost them."

"I can see that."

After a while, the driver stopped at an intersection, and the wayfarer slipped out without noticing the toothbrush that fell from one of the pockets of his jacket.

He was in the city center. Further ahead, a nice place was revealed; colorful leaves lay on the ground of a small park as nearly as wings entangled on the horizon.

> *Poetry is a language spoken between different life circles.*

Tickles

"So, these are the shoes you need…" The travel agent said when the wayfarer, somewhat tired, made a pause in the review of his memories. "I didn't know angels need shoes at all. Why? What for?"

The wayfarer shook his head. "To walk on earth by foot, that's why. Look around, to learn. Everything down here looks quite different from how it looks from above. Don't look surprised."

"Find something else; what's special about those?"

"I heard all kinds of rumors, such as the travel with these shoes is comfortable, completely unlike journeys wearing any other shoes. *Sun shines on the footprints left behind. These shoes were extremely flexible and fit every foot.* They lead you safely through unknown roads. Every shoe has a role in leading the soul to fulfill its destiny but angels' shoes take you to places never seen before. Thus, you feel like in in a dream while walking with them. Travelers, who found such pair, told about journeys to all kinds of exotic sights, views with lakes and castles…Even a forest rising in the middle of the desert."

The guy was looking at him with keen eyes. "Boy, the angel I had met in that bar, said those shoes were the best. Although he only heard it by rumors, with those shoes, the effect is probably stronger than of regular shoes. When you put them on the windowsill, not only one stone falls out from inside but a whole stream that forms a new landscape; it represents your dream. At night, a stream of stones and hot ash bursts out according to the parson's dream. The stream flows from inside them, sometimes for hours, so you can walk the new route on morning."

After a few more notes about the shoes, a point came when he was silent then nodded; he remembered something. "Among other things the long winged angels I met in the poets' village told me that there was one complication. One must be careful not to pick the shoes too soon before they are entirely empty as every stone is important and useful. If one small piece of a dream is missing in the path the shoes paved, the traveler's faith remains incomplete; his faith remains unclear…Sometimes, so they say, at the end of the path, the traveler finds a treasure."

Stretching his back at the other side of the bench, he shook his head and rose, and seemed having some difficulties standing up. "I am sure that I will feel it when I find them. It should feel incredible wearing old magic shoes. Anyway, they are the only ones that might fit me. I don't understand how I haven't found them yet. You have no idea how many shoes I have tried. I have been everywhere. I am tired," he added.

As he walked away the agent hurried to go too. His lunch break was over long ago.

Later, standing by the window of his office looking out, he saw a flock of migrating birds adorning the sky, a common sight in a city that lay by the sea. These birds seemed nearly as confused as tourists that went to a safari in the desert ending up on a ski vacation. Watching them flying above the park, he remembered the guy mentioning among other things that shoes were like birds. Why, he couldn't remember. Birds do not wear shoes; why do angels…?

They say that birds don't just sing a song, they tell a story...

They met again the next days at noon and the guy continued sharing his memories of the search. He traveled to far, small villages following rumors of old shoes found lately. The owners were surprised but usually permitted him to check their shoes solving a dream stuck within, if necessary. Each pair unfolded its unique story; mostly, of relationship and career.

None fit though.

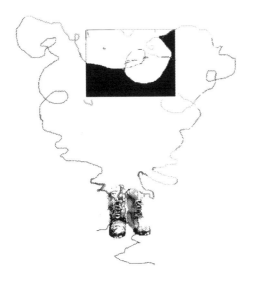

One cycle is as nearly long as the time required to learn a better technical skill and style.

Gold–Finger

It all started on the morning when the woman found a pair of shoes hanging on a tree in the backyard at her house. It wasn't clear how they got there but she pulled down the shoes. The next morning, she decided on getting into the food business. She borrowed money from her relatives to open a restaurant in the city center.

A week later, she met her cousin on the street, and she confessed that it was hard to compete with so many restaurants out there. "I don't know what to do. I cannot return to you and the others the loans. I even met a wayfarer-psychic who was ready to help in any way he could. He wanted the shoes I found. I told him, 'Why don't you cook some visions, like those who look at sea maps and point to the exact spots of sunken ships with lost treasures?'"

Her cousin sighed and his aunt continued, "I wondered if he would see a sunken ship in the near bay. Then I would be able to return the loans. I laid a map of the region on the table and his hand rose swinging above then slowly lowered, one finger pressing on some spot; but it was on land. Anyway, after the meeting was over I went to see that place…" she sighed on her turn, "An abandoned terrain outside town. I dug and dug in the ground every inch but I did not find gold. Nothing was buried there. In that case, he turned out to be a fraud."

When his aunt went her way, her cousin felt pity for her. Thus, the following invitation for dinner in her restaurant later that week came as a surprise.

They sat at one side table in the corner of the restaurant. As she poured wine into their glasses, her cousin watched the place in the light of florescent lamps slung from the ceiling. It was full with people in fancy clothes, their eyes twinkling with pleasure while eating.

He gasped at her as she wrote a check, returning the debt to him. "What happened here?" he asked.

"Magic…!" she replied. "That guy did find a treasure. I just did not see it right away. After our meeting, I told him he did not fulfill his part in the deal. I warned him that I would sue him in court for giving me false information. He did not seem bothered until I mentioned his fingerprint was embedded on the map very clearly. A solid proof. When he saw I was serious, he agreed on settling it outside court by helping in the kitchen as compensation. Ever since he joined the staff, we got compliments on the food and the place is full every night."

Her cousin drank from his wine. "He cooks well?"

"He is not cooking at all. I am. But he wears the shoes and every time he tucks his finger inside the pot to taste the food, it turns delicious. He really cooks visions, doesn't he? You ought to try the baked potatoes. They grew after all the digging in that deserted terrain."

> *A medium is the Seeing Eye of souls.*
>
> -Ocuares Mirades

A Little Touch

A farmer was waiting in the reception when the doctor entered putting a mug of coffee on the desk. With his rich résumé, the Doc could choose to work anywhere but running a clinic in the village was more interesting to him.

"I'm not a dentist," the doctor said noticing the farmer's hand cupping his mouth.

"You are the best qualification I've got, doc. I don't feel like going to the city right now." The farmer barely pronounced the words. "Octobers are not kind to my teeth. I was having a great meal. A real collunarium peak…after that the food was lying in my stomach, all I wanted was to sleep. In fact, I was already sleeping but one tooth ached, shaking up every joint in my body. This is beyond bearable."

The doctor leaned over and the farmer wide-opened his mouth. "Research done lately revealed a connection between colors and toothaches…Never mind. I'll see what I can do."

The next hour was painful but when it was over the farmer rose from his chair relieved; the tooth pain was gone. He was heading towards the door when the doc noticed that he was limping. "What's wrong with your leg?"

"It is the muscle; caught in the last couple of days. Pity, as the regional amateurs' soccer league final is this weekend. In this condition, I won't be able to play."

"Not under the normal circumstances, you won't, but I have heard that a wayfarer with certain abilities has come to our village. According the rumors, he is good. Might be able to cure your leg faster than any medicines. It is the best advice I can give you right now."

The farmer expressed his surprise to hear a person with an academic background recommend some 'healer'.

"Do not underestimate the power of alternative medicine. That's all I am saying…" The doctor added. "His methods are based on the reconstructing the soul's previous lives."

The farmer nodded, "Is it true that doctors were murderers in a previous life?"

The man in white shook his head, "I didn't expect to hear that from you. This mistake stems from different interpretations to the word 'doctor' in olden days."

Limping outside, the farmer changed direction toward the local bar thinking, 'After all, why not… if that would help me to play on Saturday.' Entering, he sat against the wayfarer, stretching his leg forward.

"Your shoes are the source of the problem; you found them recently, didn't you?" the wayfarer said after checking the farmer's shoes. "I recommend that you not use them anymore. Take them off and leave them to me. You should buy other shoes. With these shoes, a memory from a previous life somehow came up. It seems that you were a horse of an aristocrat baron in the seventeen century and you ran in the plains for many years until you were shot in the leg by someone. The mere memory of that shot caused the limp."

The wayfarer let his hand moving over the farmer's leg from waist to foot slightly touching the knee. Just a little touch it was that passed a kind of a shockwave through his leg, and the next moment the farmer was standing up on his feet as healthy as new. A few steps in the room revealed the pain was gone.

"I freed the energy of dreams, which was caught your leg. By the way, what position do you play?" the wayfarer asked.

"Defender."

"You should be a striker; run like in the old days."

"Impossible! How could I have had a previous life at all? Football wasn't even invented back then!" the farmer thought and stumbled back home. He was ready for the big match.

The playing field was located on the beach with the risk that someone might kick the ball to the sea. As the players of both teams took their places, the match began. The ball passed from side to side, each team trying to break the other's defense. Someone passed the ball to him and he started dribbling toward the post of the other team running and running, as fast as a horse carried on winds. None of the players of the opposing team could catch up with his speed. His teammates shouted, encouraging from behind. Finally, he got himself up against the goalkeeper, who was standing in his post, between the improvised net - two rocks. He kicked the ball with the full power of his leg. The goalkeeper did not bother to move and try to catch the strong kick; it was not precise enough though. The ball hit the left rock and ricocheted to the field. He blew his chance.

His disappointed teammates called, "Why did you kick so strongly? You just needed to touch the ball and you'd have scored; a touch, that's all... Just a little touch..."

A dream is a deposit and a promotion of destiny.

Be-leaf

*Belief: a direct line to the center of the universe, connecting us all as leaves of one tree…And the wind whispers through the branches: be-a-leaf… BEALEAF…**belief.***

To be reincarnated, a soul needs to climb up the tree, or the "bank of leaves", wherein each leaf weighs about three hundred grams, equaling the weight of the soul. Falling leaves represent previous lives; falling from the tree of eternity, some leaves drifting forever as footprints of angels. A second sight is the course.

The number of times we dream in our lives is equal to the number of lives we had.

Souls are fallen tears lost in the sea.

> ### *The soul is leading negotians with destiny through dreams*

Crisis

The president called for an urgent meeting concerning the growing tension in the Middle East. Some of his advisors recommended settling it down the same as the mafia handles delicate matters, by appointing a special negotiator, an outside person accepted by the sides involved in the conflict.

"Mr. President, I know the person for the job," the media advisor said.

"Who? Everybody avoids politics these days."

When the advisor whispered the name of the TV phenom, the president raised an eyebrow. "I did not know she had a flare for politics. She is totally devoted to her orphans' projects."

"Which is exactly the reason everybody would trust her," the advisor exclaimed. "Think about it, sir, we have tried only politicians until now. She is famous in the entire world. Everybody appreciates her. She is non-governmental and has neither financial nor political interest in the conflict… I heard that one Sheikh from Saudi Arabia buys only stuff which she recommends on her TV show. If any of his wives buys something else, she is excluded from his harem. I have already spoken with some of the leaders in the region. The Syrian president promised to give it a thought. The others are discussing it. And the Israelis, as always, want to see where it goes."

"Why do you suppose she would agree to accept this tough mission at all?" The president wondered.

The advisor coughed, "Because she consulted with a medium, who revealed that all the leaders in this region were orphans in their previous lives."

Application Shoe

His friend recommended the healer who was seated at the table in the corner of the bar. The healer even had a visiting card; no name on it, no address; just the word 'healer' and a logo in a form of a shoe. His friend told him that this healer has been working in the nearby towns. He helped many people to quit smoking. After the treatment, they couldn't put a cigarette in their mouth anymore. This healer said that smoking stemmed from guilt over things done in previous life cycles, and lighting a cigarette was an unconscious way of trying to 'burn' old sins. The healing process included revealing those scenes, separating them from the current life.

As the man sat down, he felt his fingers moving as if on their own fumbling in his pockets for a cigarette.

The healer requested to see his shoe.

He fumbled it for a while then held the shoe over the man's head. "A self-superior approach is the gravitation of the soul. From this day forwards, each time you fancy a cigarette, your shoe will become hot and you will have to run."

"That's it?" the man asked when the healer returned the shoe to him.

He had a job interview scheduled for later that day, for a financial advisor post; the firm would hire only nonsmokers and he had a good feeling about it even when he saw the long line of candidates in the corridor of a high floor in the building of the recruiting firm.

He entered the office on his turn facing a man who signed him to sit down; reading his CV, the man was turning the pages one by one; then he put the file down and said, "Looking at the history of your reincarnations, I think you are not qualified for the job; we'll be in touch though."

The candidate rushed out of the office; his shoe was burning.

A dream is the signature on the contract with destiny

Karma

His days started on dawn but that night he had a long dream and when he woke up, sun was riding on the horizon. He was a newspaper deliverer. Private subscribers were also in his line.

He rushed out of his flat, and entered his car but in his hurry did not notice the gear was in reverse and when he pressed the gas pedal, the car jumped backward on the pavement and hit a bench. He heard a shout and got out to see if anybody was hurt. Nobody was there though, only a pair of worn shoes lay on the bench. When he turned to go back to his car, a whisper ran through his head, *'My name is 'Karma'.*

He turned around and suddenly a rabbit jumped out of one shoe, wagging its ears.

'These shoes could be useful for winter...'

The man rubbed his forehead confused by the whisper. There was no other possibility except that this rabbit used telepathy to communicate. Perhaps the hit stressed the animal to such extent it somehow developed this ability.

"Glad to meet you...Karma." The man said "...You have a nice name but I'm late for work and you stink."

The small animal reacted with a slight nod that was beyond words. The man cupped his ears trying to block the stream flowing through his aching head.

"The stench must be a side effect of the telepathy. I just wanted to tell you that Karma means an ancient decision of nature; an old habit that never changes... It is not a coincidence that a rabbit and a turtle were the heroes of the famous race anecdote. They are symbols, two sides of the same karma. One can choose to be a turtle or a rabbit. By the way, thanks for waking me up; I was just in the middle of another race…this turtle might have been a rabbi in a previous life. I shouldn't lose again… I will win this time."

Suddenly, the rabbit looked alarmed and ran away as an escaping criminal.

"Wait," the man called but the animal ran fast as if she saw a shadow of some big hunting bird wavering on the ground. Forgetting about his work, the man followed her. He wanted her to stop the flood of unclear words, which kept running in his head…a mumble…it drove him nuts.

People passing by raised eyebrows at the man walking about, calling, "Karma, where are you? Karma…!"

A distinctive stench drifting in the air led to a block nearby. Standing by the stairways, he covered his nose and looked around but there was no sign of the rabbit. "Karma, say something…"

A feminine voice came in return. He jumped surprised and turned around. A woman climbing downstairs asked, "What is this stench?"

"It is the smell of Karma," he said as their glances locked; he felt the meeting with this pretty woman was meant to be at this time of his destiny. And silence reigned in his head.

"I *was* expecting you," the woman eventually remarked. "Where is my newspaper this morning?"

"Sold out," he said.

She explained she just wanted to read the astrology section. She couldn't make tough decisions without it.

*

The wayfarer eased backward on the bench opening a rolled newspaper that fell from one shoe. He was reading the headlines until he reached the weather section. It was going to be heavy rain for the following days.

Dream is like a 'black box', which saves data concerning the flight. Only here, the airplane is a soul to find the reasons for the crash.

Each soul buys a piece
in the puzzle of the world.

Train

She is alone in the wagon, with a paper cup in her hand, looking out of the window. As the train rolls, the blonde haired woman takes a seep and twists her face. The taste is of some kind of expensive imported coffee that she bought in the restaurant wagon at the other end of the train.

Her sight fades swallowed in the darkness of a tunnel. A big eye is reflected on the window glass, aimed at her. *The conductor…? She* fumbles in her bag to find her ticket but the eye winks out changing into a station peeping through the misty valley. She hears two women; laughs are muted by the train siren. Then two light beams flood the cabin and argue about the seat against her.

Magnificent views roll by outside. The blonde takes another swallow from her cup when a farmer carrying a basket full with red fruits enters the cabin. One fruit falls to the floor and rolls from side to side as if cannot find a free seat until it is crushed by her heel as she passes, and leaves.

When the train stops, a big crow perched on the roof of the train station sings for those who just got off. As the blonde walks along the deck, the crow flies, picks the ticket that she throws and flies away.

"I must have been on the wrong line," the crow sings preparing for a long trip.

Coaching Shoe

A house in an old-fashioned architecture in the main street. A few light beams break through the windows as solved dreams of the morning sun. A slim waitress for an hour; a cup of coffee on the table. One customer inside; he takes off one shoe letting the wayfarer fumble it. "These are the last word in the sport shoe market, made of a very sophisticated material, very flexible, worth every dime. Feel for yourself."

On his rich experience, the wayfarer knew that athletic shoes needed more time to 'speak up'. As he laid it on the windowsill, a few red roofs broke through the morning mist across the street, and he said, "The shoe tells me about an important match next week."

"The regional finals;" The customer cleared his throat… As the coach of the local school's basketball team, he was worried as the other team was better.

The wayfarer nodded. "Each team member is like a fuse. If the all fuses are on, the team wins. One short fuse, and the team loses. Your role is to be the intermediary and balance between abilities and expectations."

"How?"

"Train the kids in the darkness. Let them throw the ball without seeing the basket, to improve intuition and coordination. Intuition is the muscle of the soul. After such training, the kids will have less air ball and the so-called blind-shots would be precise, easy and smooth. Seeing the hoop is not required. The precision of a shot depends on energy, which the ball gets from the hands in the quality of the intention… Tell the kids to think positively when they throw the ball, to imagine that the basket is a mother wishing to hug her child. They must think that they do not just throw a ball but let a bird go free from a cage. The ring is not a challenge for the ball, but a positive extension of energy... a ball falling into the ring is like a little dream coming true. Then, the scorer and the crowd in the hall feel as part of one dream as if a spell passes from one parson to another.

"When all the fuses work, the souls of the players rise and mingle into one big eye that sees the arena from above. Then, every player knows exactly where the other is, each moment of the game and all act as one unit. Each does the right thing during the match, a move that can change the momentum. And it is not necessarily a virtuous dunk, far shot, or a block. It can be a short pass or just standing in a certain spot in the court. It is all about timing. The right timing is a message from an angel."

The wayfarer was silent; he knew the shoe was solved when in the misty street emerged an old woman carrying a basket full up to top with fruits.

> *City shines in the distance,*
> *a village is on fire.*

Homemade Memo

A heavy mist lay outside almost hiding the fancy car that was parked near the bar. The owner, a young farmer was sitting against the wayfarer.

He had a successful specialty dairy business, and by the age of twenty, he was one of richest farmers in the country. His secret, he said, was using only homemade stuff; he made everything by himself; even his clothes, from the shoes to the hat; he built alone his house and fixed his car with his two hands.

Lately he had dreams for which he had been weakening in a sweat, a recurring dream of a car accident. Could it be a warning? What did he do to deserve these dreams?

Sitting against the wayfarer, he had a mixture of naivety and wariness in the eyes.

"I don't know anything about warnings," the wayfarer said checking the farmer's fancy shoe. "Let your shoes lead you if you want to solve this dream; drive in the same road where the accident happened."

The farmer followed the advice. As soon as he entered his fancy car, the dream seemed to steer him far from the village, toward a highway from which forests stretched on both sides. After a few hours, he drove by the sea, the playing field of wild winds and angels. That moment, the farmer pulled over. His hands shook on the steering wheel as in the rear-view mirror, an unshaven face covered by blood appeared much clearly now… the car accident scenes… a wounded man in an ambulance…a woman, perhaps the wife standing by his hospital bed…

He drove off in the dark; city lights in the distance stirred in his heart an odd longing.

Dusk: a jam of trolleys, buses, and cars against the backdrop of huge billboards in the city center. His dream was leading him away from downtown, to a street where the apartment blocks all looked alike. Never the less, he recognized one, parked the car, and descended the stairs until he stopped in the third floor staring at the sign on the door.

"'Wayne'", it said. He had heard that name somewhere before... a teakettle whistling as he rang the bell. The same wife from the visions, much older though, opened the door. He chose to say that he was a salesman; he showed her a small bottle he had picked from the baggage trunk of the car, a sample of his firm's product. She invited him inside.

He plopped on the sofa like someone who'd had an exhausting day, struggling against the strong wish to hug her. It wasn't so unusual as every now and then he had a wish to hug stranger. But when the teakettle she set down on the coffee table reflected images of her husband — the man who had appeared in the rear-view mirror, he knew there was something else.

The question was: Was he Mr. Wayne in a previous life? He wondered about it as she told him about her husband. He'd emerged from the war without a scratch. But he'd been over-confident on the roads, and one day on the way home, he lost control of the car. The police believed it had been a mechanical failure. He was rushed to the hospital, but it was soon over.

Listening to her, he let his fingers play absently with the red silky laces slung from the side of the sofa, but he stopped when he noticed a tear rolling down her cheek, and realized that her late husband used to engage in the same habit.

"I run a farm and I drive a lot to sell our products. We make goat's milk products." He removed from his pocket the bottle although he wasn't sure of its quality after the long drive. "It's organic, based on a traditional recipe."

Handing it to her, his eyes drooped.

Mrs. Wayne brought a blanket, covered him up, and retired to her bedroom. The guest felt at home. He must be tired after such a long drive, she thought.

Silence fell over the apartment and moonlight through the window threw a profile of his face onto the wall opposite.

On awakening, he brushed his hair and washed his face. Nothing more refreshing than cold water after a long night's sleep. He wore some old pants that she had left in the living room.

Mrs. Wayne was still asleep. He left a short note, just "Thank you", and left.

Outside, he searched in his pockets for the keys. Deep inside one pocket, he found a yellowed piece of paper. It appeared to be an old receipt for the car's remounts.

He entered the car, whose odor suddenly annoyed him. He had made it from pieces of different old cars.

A few miles outside of town, his foot ached from pressing on the gas pedal. He took off one shoe, and shook it through window until a stone fell outside. A little dream it was. The farmer enjoyed the rest of the drive back home.

*

On awakening, she stood by the window, finishing the yogurt that her guest had left. It was sower but tasty. It reminded her of the phone call she'd received from her late husband during his last drive; just before the accident, he'd promised her he'd bring milk home.

…Just before his eyes closed.

Memory is a prisoner of time; freedom is second sight.

Recipe

Standing by the window in the top floor looking out, the travel agent saw the small exceptional figure of the barefoot being down below, in the park across the road. He grabbed some coffee and rushed outside, even though some paperwork lay on his desk since morning.

They met in the park almost every day over the past week – and each time the guy would sit down, stretch his legs forward and tell him a story of another pair he had found.

Not today. "I'm tired," the wayfarer sighed. "I don't know how long I'll be able to stay. Just this morning, I took a trip to visit another village, with no results. I guess that is why some call them track shoes. One needs to track them down. I wonder if those shoes exist at all. But the rumors say that one pair was found and the evidence all point to this region. Just hope that if they had fallen in the sea, they were washed to shore. The foam of the waves is nearly as old as angels."

A moment of silence passed as the wayfarer bent forward and scratched his foot.

"You may find them one day," the travel agent tried to encourage him, rubbing his hands to warm up.

"Who knows?" He was rising from the bench, his gaze fixed on a fancy car passing in the street.

"There are some stores you might have missed," the agent said. "I figured that since angels' shoes were ancient, they might be in antique stores."

The wayfarer's face lightened up. "I suppose so; it's worth checking out. They might be in such sort of place lying among antique merchandise. Could have been brought there after some clumsy angel had lost them."

The travel agent just gently nodded in agreement, his gaze following the figure lurching through the shadows across the park. It was a mystery where that guy was sleeping.

His lunch break was over. Meetings with clients about their organized tours were calling him; among others, the old couple who were interested in the South Pacific Cruise. They had more questions.

*

Far from there, the wayfarer stood on a big square known for its many fancy lavish shopping windows but down the street, one shopping window at the bottom of a building looked different, somewhat pale among the other stores. As he paused, standing against that shopping window, it looked like a television screen with the street's reflections merging with the items for sale within. The reflection of his figure in a weary jacket fit in among dusty old things of all kinds lying there. It turned out to be an antique store. No doubt, this was the kind of place where he should have been searching for angels' shoes from the start. After all, shoes should fit one's clothes.

He had to wait though because the seller was on a break. When he returned at last, the wayfarer asked him, "Do you have angels' shoes?"

The latter frowned then fumbled in the back carrying one pair with a worn, stained, old look, but that seemed well preserved. "I have only this pair."

Shrugging, the wayfarer picked them. At first, he was not sure it was a pair at all since they were a bit different from one another.

"You may have come to the wrong place if you are looking for shoes to wear; this is an antique from the Middle Ages; all I know is it belonged to famous parson, a real hero," the old seller notified the barefoot customer, who settled down on some silver wooden box from the Renaissance, trying to tuck his foot into one shoe, the right one perhaps.

It was tight; a dream was stuck within. And when he took off the shoe and fumbled it, the dream ran shivers down his arm, taking him farther than ever before; visions of a different time and place rose up one after the other around him, featuring the previous owner a long time ago in some small kingdom.

He remembered that often while shaking a shoe longer before, an old period from the owner's life was revealed, even a previous life. He remembered once checking one barman's shining shoe that featured a sailor sailing in the heart of the sea on an old kind of boat that dated back to previous centuries. That scene was from the barman's previous life.

"That man had a strong, big soul..." The wayfarer said with a full picture in his mind with many spicy ingredients. The owner appeared to be a knight. He was wounded in one tough battle, and while recovering he spent his time learning cooking. Knives replaced the sword, the kitchen became the battlefield. He made a reputation and became the royal chef in a small kingdom. His dinners were culinary feasts but there were times he went over the limit with spices and threw into the pot whatever he found in the kitchen, meat, seafood, and witches' sauces, as his motto was that food should not be thrown away. Leftovers from one meal became the dessert of the next, and the opposite.

On evenings, high official guests sat at the king's table but no one was able to guess the ingredients of the meals. Some described his cooking kitschy; others thought it to be exotic. While eating, some of the dinning guests seemed like fish swimming among bread thrown into the aquarium.

Fumbling lower, reaching to the sole, the wayfarer saw the reason why the knight had become a chef. In a previous life, he was involved with this woman but they had to keep their relationship a secret. Perhaps she was married...so, he sent her love letters in code as recipes. Each food ingredient stood for a different word and expression. Different vegetables and fruits for good and bad feelings. 'Spices' was her nickname. Some letters found by mistake won popularity considered revolutionary in the cooking world at that time. In the next life of a knight, the wayfarer said, he became a chef so that he could find the soul of that woman again.

He was good, and even the king joked about it saying that his chef was the real king in the kingdom. He did not wish to fire him but some of the servants wanted to quit as they couldn't eat the food. He tried to talk to him more than once explaining that he could not put garlic in cakes, and that oranges did not go together with avocado or artichoke in a salad. Yet nothing changed; the chef claimed that he was more than just a cook, but an artist; every meal was a masterpiece. He used cooking in a 'Dutch Pot', a pot that is never cleaned. The leftovers of every food cooked inside mix with a new one, as in a reincarnation; any new life circle gets a few elements from the previous one.

One day, a duke from a far country passed by and decided to stay with his family for the night, see what the fuss was all about. The specialties that evening were beyond imagination and nobody succeeded finishing the food. Only one plate remained empty; the plate of the duke's beautiful daughter.

A few days later, the chef announced on his engagement to her; he prepared the food for the wedding by himself a week ahead.

The happy couple opened the ceremony with a dance to which, counts, princes from other countries, and a few known Russian aristocrats joined one after the other.

"What does a beautiful girl like her see in him?" The king said and picked up from the buffet a kind of fried ball. The queen explained to her husband that those two were probably soul mates. One does not choose a soul mate, as a nation does not choose a king. Destiny is an inheritance of the soul. She had sensed something was going on between them at that dinner. No wonder the daughter ate as if it was the best food she has ever had. There must have been something in the food or she is simply a glutton as she was only one who finished it. Food prepared by the soul brings love back. Could be they had met each other in a previous life for which the food touched her soul…

"By cooking, he seemed to have found the way back to her heart."

"If you say so," the king said spitting the food out of his mouth. "All I know is she has got no taste."

*

The seller was busy wiping patiently some dust from a vase clad in a glistening mosaic mounted in a pseudo-classical plinth.

When the wayfarer ended his study, he turned the shoe upside down and a much folded wrapped yellowish piece of paper slid out. He unfolded it carefully and a glamorous diamond was revealed glistening in his eyes. The seller picked out the shining stone whilst the wayfarer looked at the note, trying to make something out of the words in handwriting.

– 'Lucky Tunes' –

(A recipe for 'I miss you. When shall I see you again?')

> *Gum*
> *Yellow pees*
> *Cranberries*
> *Artichoke*

Mash everything together, then create small balls, and throw them into each other's mouth.

After reading that, the wayfarer put on the shoe again and pleasant vibrations tickled down at his feet; he made a few steps across the store. Although the footsteps sounded with annoying creaks, they felt more comfortable than anything else he had tried until then. In fact, it seemed they were made especially for him. Only as he passed the doorstep, the hardness of the soles made him feel as if he was walking on rocks. It bothered him more than the creaks. No choice did he have but to leave the shoes in the store.

Anyway, he was trying to get over his disappointment by looking for another antique shop that was supposed to be down the street.

When he requested from the seller to see the oldest shoes he had, the latter fumbled behind some old paintings in the corner and brought a rather worn pair. A tag, which read $200, was attached to the toe of one shoe but it did not bother the wayfarer. As his foot was inside, he felt like falling, drowning by visions, and it unfolded upon him its previous life - the travels of the previous owner, with the beauty of days that used to be. When he fumbled the shoes from top to bottom, from shoelaces to soles, a dream ran shivers down his arm. There was a knight waving with his sword to cut a way through a thick forest. When he cut another tree, a baby fell down from the top but it did not reach the ground. It just floated among the trees and showed the knight a way out of the forest.

"That knight must have expected a tough battle," the wayfarer said.

After the dream was solved, a shining flash came from within one shoe and a tiny shiny stone slipped outside. It was a blue sapphire, a high-rated stone in the spiritual circles. First the diamond and now this. It taught him that precious stones came as a result of dreams that were stuck in shoes for a long time. However, the shoes didn't fit.

But once, when he entered another antique shop and found an old-looking pair and solved a dream, an ordinary piece of wood dropped out which told him the shoes were not a real antique at all but a few years old at the most, a fraud. The shop owner was a liar.

In another shop, he thought he would be able to run with the shoes he found there, but the comfortable old hessians tore apart to pieces at the second step.

He stood on the corner outside considering where to go next when a familiar melody was cutting through the street. Up on the roof, a bird was singing in style. It seemed to be the same bird he had heard in one village before. One last chord before it flew away made him feel a bit better after the last failures. He watched its small shadow fluttering rapidly on the ground farther and farther like a telegram… until lost from sight…and he wondered again what inspired that bird and what defined its course.

Perhaps it saw musical notes on the ground. Perhaps the footprints of the old shoes he had just checked in that boutique looked like notes from above. Could he find nice old shoes by following singing birds? There must be other melodies and compositions written on the ground by footprints of travelers, footprints seen as notes through the bird eye. Obviously, footprints left by old shoes inspired birds the most. One composition might come from the particular shoes he needed.

And so, following birdsongs over the next weeks, he was hoping to find nice old shoes. He listened to tweeters and whistlers and each time the twits were with unique bits and chords, he followed the composition until the bird landed silently, knowing somewhere nearby might be some old, used shoes. Different birds landed on house roofs of different people, of a baker, a postman, a surgeon, politician. One bird landed near a stripper. Some birds flew farther than others, to the far ends of the countryside. He met the shoe owner at the end of each song and the shoes were indeed promising although none fit.

At least twice, he felt so comfortable with pairs that seemed his size that he tried to fly with them. When he rose in the air though, the shoes slipped off his feet, which would not have occurred with real angel's shoes to the best of his knowledge.

There were other complications. Some birds led to shoes in a terrible state thrown at the sides of the roads or, on someone's feet, travelers and other people, some not willing to let him check their shoes so easily and he had to be a bit more persuasive.

Footprints of a traveler are notes in the songs of the birds. Irregular mountains are the chorus.

Matthew H Yin

After Party – Politics shoe

The bird was singing a nice melody flying farther and farther until it rested on a chimney of an old fancy house. The wayfarer was wandering around in one of the suburbs until he found it, and knocked on the door hoping the owner would be open-minded enough to let him check his shoes.

The vice chair parson of the local labor party was not the typical type of politician. He played the guitar and wrote poetry. As the main candidate for the leader post in the present elections, he prepared a speech to the slightest detail. He even consulted with the wayfarer, who checked his shoes and assured him that he would win.

The official party hall was being remodeled so they hired another hall specifically for the elections conference later that week. Each of the candidates was sure of his leadership qualities and long speeches spilled out one after the other, in an evening in which many dreams were on the verge to come true. The vice chairperson was the last to go upstage.

Whistling and shouting followed as soon as he started his speech. Reporters reviewing the event said it was like a market. People called in a demand and he would step down, giving a chance to others, people that are more talented.

On he carried though.

Dear friends,
On these rough days,
Our party needs a brave leader!
Choose me and we shall rise!
Every voice counts.
Every vote is a kiss.
And the future hugs us!

The whistles went louder and longer as youngsters seated in the first rows tried to explain to him that the party hired the hall only for two hours, which were over. A new event was about to begin, an amateurs singing contest. The crowd changed into singers who waited to go on stage and give their number. It was not clear if he understood, still reading, committed to his ideas under any circumstances. One friendly face found in the back rows encouraged him. The fan, who clapped excitedly to every word, turned to be a member of the jury. "This is exactly what I am looking for in this contest," the judge said; "a star is born! I hear passion, a stand, the voice of the unskilled labor protesting against the capitalist world and the music industry. Had he led a political party, I would have voted for him! I have faith that this ambitious guy can reach the finals. I am passing him to the next stage of this competition."

A dream is a rapport the soul gets when it passes the limited speed.

Hair Salon & the Gardener's Shoe

A couple of days passed with no particular birdsongs registered across the sky. The wind whistled a solo, until a bird with yellow-edged wings and sharp eyes whistled high and far, flying to the edge of the countryside, touching a cloud. For a moment, the cloud seemed to sing to the snowy tops cropping up, until the bird flew downward, landing on the irregular escarpments of the mountain.

Perched on a house in a village, twittering a chorus, the bird looked tired. The wayfarer hasn't arrived yet, left far behind.

The owner of the house, a tall woman was checking on the flowers in the garden; as she bent over a lovely white rose, a pair of shoes thrown on the ground caught her eye. Could be the work shoes of her gardener, who had worked there a month ago; *he had either forgotten them, or just had thrown them away,* she thought and picked them. As she entered inside the house, and put the shoes on the table, suddenly, a mirror hung on the wall creaked. She turned around. The looking glass shone tingling her face in blue. In the mirror, the sky stretched forth with gray clouds from which a flying carpet emerged, ridden by a creature with two narrow, devil's eyes; he was wearing a long, fancy cap flying in the wind. Blinking about the room, he noticed the pair of shoes on a table among scattered fashion magazines.

He turned to her, with a tight glance from the mirror "Give me these shoes and I'll make your wish come true. I need them to get out of the mirror. I have tired flying on a carpet."

Cecilia – that was her name, was a bit shocked by his appearance. "I've always dreamed of having my own hair-saloon," she said studying the oriental ornamentation of the carpet.

"No problem," the creature said. "I can handle that. You just bring the clients. I'll **make the mirror** more than an ordinary mirror. It will reflect a hairdo that suits the customer, and you will just cut and style according to that. Nothing is more aesthetic, spiritual and authentic than a hairdo from a previous life."

She made some calls to her friends and her neighbors and soon, the first client, a blond woman arrived, seated curiously on a chair opposite the wide mirror on the wall.

Her reflection slowly changed until another woman with a different face and hairdo looked back, which was odd, as their motions were identical. The woman in the mirror wore an old-fashioned hairdo with black Russian corkscrew curls, but the blond customer uttered approvingly, "That is exactly what I wanted."

The tall house owner picked up her shears, bent a bit behind the customer and cut the hair to match the reflection in the mirror. The floor looked like a lawn of yellowed grass as she finished.

The client beamed as she rose, letting another woman just entering take the seat and face the mirror, anticipating the metamorphosis. Her reflection changed into another woman with a different hairdo. "The client is always right. Everybody knows what she's getting," Cecilia said.

The creature fulfilled his part in the deal. One after another, clients indeed arrived, and a group of women stood in line at the entrance. Customers were coming from all over the region. A sign on the door read "Cecilia's Salon".

The Soul Mirror displayed changing faces throughout the day. Skepticism was replaced by discovery of previous lives. Fabulous hairdos exited the salon. There still seemed to be misunderstandings, as some did not want the hairdo in the mirror wonderful as it was, as it differed so widely from any criterion of aesthetic in recent decades.

Occasionally two visages popped up, and the client had to choose between them. Other clients waited for several minutes, but the reflection didn't change. The creature decreed they did not need a new do, or that they'd had no previous life.

An elderly couple entered, the woman fearfully sitting on her husband's knees. They exited looking like seventies rockers singing 'The Rising sun'.

One teenager saw an old woman in the mirror. Another teenager saw a white mouse, running on a wheel and as she ran outside in tears, the mouse ran ever faster until it faded.

After a few more clients, the creature suddenly reappeared, his polite firm voice cutting through the mirror, "Now I want the shoes. They're mine…"

He stretched a hand with long and sharp nails, reaching out for the shoes"…Mine."

Eventually, he lost his balance and fell off the carpet, waving his hands in the air. A shout echoed behind the mirror glass, fading as the figure fell out of sight.

When the image vanished, Cecilia called the next client.

The wayfarer entered the room; the scent of hair gel met him; he was unable to take his eyes off the worthy shoes that rested near the fashion magazines.

"You certainly look like you need a haircut about now," Cecilia said pointing to the wide mirror on the wall.

"I thought it was a bar," the wayfarer hedged, noticing a dried blade of grass popping out of one of the shoes.

Having no choice, he sat down, and when she finished, his long white hair and beard looked as if they'd been blown about by a strong wind.

A punkish hairstyle would suit him, the hairdresser mused.

After that, she allowed him to inspect the shoes. But the blade of grass had grown, extending out the window and over a wall.

He asked the hairdresser to grasp the shoe while he pulled and tugged with both hands until the grass blade loosened and fell away. He was able to put them on now; no match though. Not his. Nothing but another false alarm.

Clients still gathered near the entrance admiring one anothers' retro hairdos as he walked away, passing others just having arrived, but turning around disappointed when they heard the salon had closed. It happened after the owner decided to clean the mirror. As she moved the rag in circular motions, a flock of birds popped up, flying in scissor formation from one side of the mirror to another, until they all flew off as in a dream… With that, the mirror settled down to normal; reflections never changed again. Her career was over.

> *A dream is a long shortcut of destiny.*

Karma of Tea

The wind was shivering the windows with some hesitations before it entered through the threshold; it was a steamy tiny bar known to a chosen few. The wayfarer led the way among the tables, although he was not sure if the birdsong had ended or the bird he had followed just decided to rest on the roof.

One young woman sitting alone caught his eyes, her long hair mussed as if she had a battle with the pillow last night... The small shoes implied a big soul. A glimpse of emergency rose on faces of farmers nearby as he sat down at the chair against her. Slightly surprised at first, she removed a curl that slid over her forehead like a frown then leaned forward and picked his hand up inspecting it with the precision of a gypsy woman looking at a map of Eastern Europe.

"I don't see stations, no stops; just travel in your life," she finally said, poured into a cup an aromatic herbal tea from a small teakettle, and handed it over to him.

The youngster was a daughter of immigrants, married to a local, a second year student in the university. She had a hobby, hand-reading. It helped paying the bills. For a short period, she tried to be a matchmaker.

"When a customer comes over, and I hold his hand, I see a vision in my mind, the face of the soul mate, his or hers. But without a name or an address and I cannot not find the person with that face. Thus, I have changed careers to a real-estate agent lately. People move in and out all the time. One needs a psychic to find a good apartment in the city. A customer comes over and when I look at his hand, the lines show me the neighborhood that fits him."

She drank from her tea. "One customer could not find a room for a long time. He wanted a nice place just to feel at home. I told him there must have been some teaser that delayed his destiny. Reading his hand, I took the man to the suburbs, and showed him a poor room. The man said it was too far from the city center but he changed his mind the moment a woman living in the next room entered. I sensed a strong chemistry between them. It was a match. Today, they live together. Sometimes, you look for one thing and you find another."

"Go to school instead of fooling around," remarked a few farmers who heard her. "One needs to study for years until they are qualified as a hand reader."

A chilling red color came to her cheeks. "That's right; the lines are a map of the soul that shakes hands with destiny. Each line portrays a spiritual level... Shaking the left hand stirs the past; the right hand shakes up the future. Two for the price of one, as the past and the future go hand in hand. The lines on a hand are parabolas of the parson's destiny. A handshake feels like a train travel with many stations. That is why I enjoy holding hands with my husband. His soul traveled a lot and he had many life circles. In one old life circle a long time ago, he was a son of a Pharaoh...

After one's death, the soul skips to another body, the same as passengers getting on and off at every station and the train keeps going with new ones. Each soul takes with it something to the next life... memories chiseled on the hand as lines."

As she looked over the bar registering no will for her service, she picked up the wayfarer's hand again. She measured one line with interest. There was a far look in her eyes as she let go of his hand. "With you, it felt like travel on the express train."

On his turn, the wayfarer pulled her hand. First, he kissed it, coughing from a distinctive stench of tobacco; then asked to see her shoe. All the eyes in the room turned to him.

Waves of compassion came in bursts as a child's cry as he fumbled the small and black shoe.

She said that she tried for a long time to get pregnant. "Do you suppose I failed because I intend to call my son Johnny?"

"Nothing wrong with that name unless it is supposed to be a girl." He fumbled the shoe again with the precision of an art critic. "I don't see any reason for the failure; I see your dream… birds crying like kids, a sign for many souls in line for a reincarnation," he uttered. "There is something else."

She frowned. "In my dream, the birds perched on the roof of an old church in some narrow street in a foreign city. Then my mom who passed away years ago comes out from inside the church in a rush. Is it some kind of a message?"

"I don't know anything about messages. But maybe your mother wants to see you happy." The wayfarer finished his tea that was quite bitter, and rose up. On his way to the door he added. "Perhaps the relationship with your husband needs work although you two are meant to be together as your names are written in heaven side by side. Try changing your approach. Do with him things he likes."

"He just wants me to go with him to a Steven Segal's movie," the youngster murmured.

Weeks later, the wayfarer entered that bar again to have a cup of tea; the hand reader was pregnant. The proud future motehr filed his cup and it was the sweetest tea he ever had. She told him that she added a lemon juice; she had plucked the lemons from a tree after she had heard a bird singing from the top of that tree; the bird could have been the reincarnated spirit of her mother, who was happy about the pregnancy.

The wayfarer asked if she still read hands; she said that she wanted to, but every time she picked someone's hand, her stomach ached as the baby inside her started moving. The baby girl - the name was chosen – Jen, would not stop waving her small hands energetically, as Steven Segal would - he was a great, true hand reader.

From then on, she quitted reading hands waiting to hold her baby's hand. The only hand that mattered now.

The soul has the same role toward dreams as parents have toward their kids.
Same as kids, some grow up, others not, only few dreams are fulfilled.

Missing

He needed a rest before picking up the trail of another birdsong from afar, carried by the wind. Sitting by the window in one roadside diner, he ordered pancakes though but the waitress, a little girl brought a deep ceramic bowl. "You ought to try our soup. It is by a traditional family recipe," she muttered, laying on the table a small plate of croutons that came in addition.

She sat against him in a wait to hear his opinion but he couldn't eat as the soup seemed too hot, a heavy steam rising from it; he tried to spread the steam waving his hand. Through the steam, he noticed at the other side of the table the print of a woman's face stretched all over the girl's T-shirt. The woman seemed smiling.

"I know what is missing," the girl said and turned on the radio that lay on the near shelf. A thrilling voice sounded in the room and even the soup bubbled in excitement.

"Don't you like Beyoncé?" the girl cried. "She is incredible, what a voice. They say she is not just singing, she is speaking with angels."

Two pigeons perched wing to wing on the window of the bar sang an acoustic version of the song. As the girl shared with them the croutons on the table, the wayfarer noticed an enigmatic smile stretched all over the mouth of the pop singer's face.

Extreme Offer

"A precious stone is a result of a dream that remained unsolved for a very long time." The wayfarer mentioned another case with a diamond that fell from inside a shoe he found at the beach. This dream was of a young woman who lived in the old days when only men used to climb to the tops of mountains. She found some worn track shoes and she became a cliff climber, an autodidact, not bred in the traditions of mountaineering but still gaining reputation. Paintings of her standing on the highest tops of the world were in many houses. She used to wear diamond-studded pants, which shone brightly from the peaks she reached. And she looked like a falling star when she fell from one peak because of a loosened rope. After the tragic accident, her soul kept climbing shining brightly, up on the highest peak ever, the next reincarnation.

*

The man stood still against one shopping window and gasped inside. Finding a shirt he really liked was as nearly as rare as finding a secret treasure. The color was perfect, the size too. He entered to the shop and tried the shirt, an import from abroad, so the seller explained.

He paid and walked away wearing the shirt, his eyes twinkling with pleasure. Down the street, he entered into a nice coffee shop and sat in the corner with a glass of juice. He felt great. Everything around seemed wonderful.

A few minutes later, a young woman entered and asked if the seat near him was free. They passed the time talking. She turned to be a member of extreme sports club; bungee and track in far countries were her favorites.

They kept seeing each other but she said she wanted to stay just friends.

He didn't give up and went to see the wayfarer who said that practicing extreme sports was a way to pay a 'debt' from a previous life. When the man wondered what she had done, the wayfarer mentioned couple of possibilities among which was escaping from a wedding at the last moment...

After that, he visited her at her place. He saw a pair of old track shoes near the door. She mentioned finding them on the top of a high mountain in her last expedition. Who knows what they have been through...As he held one shoe, suddenly, he felt as in a bungee above a deep chasm. From one of the shoes a golden ring fell on the floor.

She picked the ring, and, "Marriage is the one extreme sport I haven't tried yet."

With that, his shirt seemed to change color like a flower from destiny.

> *Following dreams; the extreme sport of the souls.*

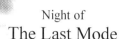

Night of
The Last Mode

"I see you found something." The travel agent was glad to see his acquaintance seated on the bench. A whole week passed since their last meeting.

The wayfarer nodded excitedly waving two ordinary-looking walk shoes. "I found them this morning, following a bird which rested on the plastic bench in one bus station. They don't fit though. You think there is a dream stuck within?"

The shoes looked almost new but the travel agent said, "I suppose so."

"I'm on it. They might become more comfortable if I solve it;" starting right away, the wayfarer fumbled each shoe, from the shoelaces to the sole.

"It's a model's dream," he murmured.

A breeze came from the sea playing with the shoelaces while he unfolded the dream.

*

The wait for the bus was not going to be short judging by the long line of people near the station. A few people were seated on a plastic bench. Among them, one old woman, who spoke on her cellular; she did yoga exercises, waving with her hands in the air, moving the toes of her feet; back straightened up, three long deep breaths.

A man next to her sat engrossed in contemplations.

Next to him, a pretty young woman looked impatiently at her watch.

A street dog just arrived, sniffing two shoes thrown by someone in the corner of the station.

People kept coming. The bus arrived at last and the young man rose from the bench. Not the women;, the youngster was unable to lay her eyes off a large advertisement placard hung all over the side of the bus, see what she could see. The text above read, **'Our jewels make whole the difference'**. It featured a model with diamond-studded jewels, bracelets, and necklaces hung on her body all over. The hair, the ears, and the nose were perfect, probably passed under the hands of a copywriter, who thought Photoshop was the invention of the century. The model seemed naked judging by the navel peeping through the precious stones.

She could have become a model herself, the youngster thought. A model with an overseas career does not need the public transport; a private limo provided by her agency takes her everywhere. She even had this dream once; she was walking with a fancy mink coat on the podium, posing in a fashion show.

When she rose from her seat, the street dog stopped playing with the shoes, and barked at her until she climbed up the packed bus.

When it drove off, creeping along the boulevard, the dog watched the placard; the navel of the model seemed shining brightly under the jewels hung on her body.

The old woman who decided to wait for the next bus stared at the dog as he walked away from the station as proudly as a model in a show of the latest mode.

> *Souls are models in the fashion*
> *show of destiny.*

*

The wayfarer ended his study, swinging with the shoes again, until a bit of sand seeped outside from one shoe. "It's not the entire dream. The other shoe is too heavy; but it doesn't matter."

Unsatisfied, he looked at the pile formed at his feet saying these shoes were not what he needed if all they could do was a bit of sand. "I was wondering why anyone would throw away new shoes."

The travel agent threw a curious glance at the pair that lay between them on the bench; a slight breeze quivered the shoelaces. Finally, he picked up the other shoe. "Do you mind…?" He started shaking it. A smile froze on his face as something dropped from within it falling down on the ground. It was a cotton ball that rolled opening into a long tinny silky line. As it was drifting in the wind farther and farther from the park along the boulevard, the wayfarer said this was a solved dream that came into existence.

"Angels' shoes can do a bit more than cotton and sand," he declared wearing the shoes just to prove his point that this pair was not his size anyway.

He bent down, scooped some sand and let it seep between his fingers as if it would give an answer as to the result of his search. Would it end successfully, or not? He was recalling things lately, he said — stuff from above followed by a tingling on his shoulder. Homesickness? Yet his wings weren't yet ready even though his clothing felt different.

With evening fallen over the park, a few windows of the tall buildings and shopping windows on the boulevard were lit. The travel agent looked at his watch wondering how to explain his absence from work that entire afternoon at the office tomorrow.

The wayfarer was quiet, rising from the bench, "Perhaps I'll see you tomorrow."

"You need a ride somewhere?"

"No. I'll walk."

Nothing else seemed fit to say. Nothing left to do.

As the other left, the travel agent was strolling toward his car that was parked near his office. Past the corner, he turned around but the latter already merged off somewhere in the shadows of the park, gone.

The city center was still very lively as he drove off to his suburb flat.

An hour later, the travel agent looked out of the window at the darkness beyond the shining city. He had a feeling he won't be seeing that guy again. Things he was saying entered into his memory as he lay in his bed; wondering... how with all of his experience as a shoe reader, he hadn't yet found shoes that would lift him?

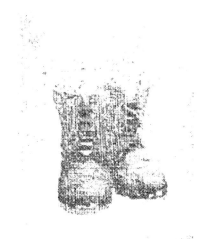

Two left

Leaving the park, the wayfarer considered where to go next. He stood near a few phone booths across the street looking down at the feet of those exiting, one after another. One individual sat on the ground outside the booth, cross-legged, holding the phone whose wire extended from inside. He had a heavy Asian accent and while speaking he swung his free hand as if attempting to fly off.

Through the melee of cars, something else reached him, weak at first: A birdsong emerged from somewhere among the tall buildings. No bird he knew of sang like that.

He moved from one street to another, to pick up the trail of the birdsong from afar, carried by the wind. Following the song, he reached the suburbs via the garages and warehouses of the industrial district; he walked down the winding route into the countryside when unexpectedly, the song ended.

It wasn't far, still inside the city limits. A mile farther, by the sea, he walked along a beach drenched in a heavy mist; he glimpsed a bird circling the water silently, as if searching for drowned notes, one wing fading, the other rising, barely detectable. The mist painted the beach gray.

"Fly after me..." A song, yes; but not a bird singing: an MP3 sounded the metallic voice of a rapper accompanying the footfalls of a jogger: "How can the politicians / Look us in the eyes? / All they care about is / Ruining the opponent's rep..."

The music fades along with the footsteps. He gropes his way; still can't see more than a few yards ahead; but faint silhouettes appear passing by one, then the other: Vague figures of ducks walking straight forward, as if following footprints on the sand. Their owner was nowhere in sight.

A surreal picture is revealed as their eyes pop open in various sizes, colors, and shapes: Ellipse-shaped, round, shining, blinking as if seeing each other for the first time. Astonishment prevails. Two pairs approach slowly until entangled in a single romantic bubble. Two other pairs look at each other as strangers, a shining ball behind them. A tear... another tear glides...tear crying over tear, rolling on the ground in crashes, dispersing into a wave.

His vision clears. He watches the ducks walk onto the main street of one of those neighborhoods around the city; a complex system of narrow lanes, endless curved terraces hanging over brick houses, and small rosy gardens.

A lit square lays ahead — the window of a barroom.

*

Sitting in the local bar, the customers were in the middle of a discussion about recent changes in the corn market and their effect on local farms.

Suddenly a howl came from nowhere, and a small gray cat landed on a chair near the table, almost as if he were about to join in the discussion. Staring at the nearby window, his eyes glowed with the liberty of two meteors. There were two shoes occupying the window box, their toes pointing inward toward the room. This window box was his favorite preserved spot, where he would watch the night sky for hours. A twinkle here, a twinkle there, with incredible combinations of starlight, the mascots of the universe. But not now, not with those shoes sitting there. What made them so important that they deserve a window box?

While the gray pet seemed to be fighting the temptation to play with the shoelaces, the bar owner approached, placing cups of tea on the table.

One of the customers, nicknamed Wind, was rising from his chair, pulling his pants above his waist. "When was this cup washed in the last time? How long has it been in the kitchen?"

"Don't worry," the landlady protested, cleaning the nearby window with a rag she had just pulled out of her pocket. Her long black curls waved from one shoulder to the other as she passed over the windowpane from left to right without missing a beat. She tried brushing the shoes, but unsuccessfully - they still looked as old, worn and dusty as when she found them while walking on the nearby beach a few weeks ago and she'd decided to keep them as décor in her bar. The exception for their forlorn state was the shoelaces, which were flecked in beautiful shades of orange and violet. They flowed out the window, almost falling on the ground outside, yet they appeared completely out of place and time. No one had noticed these shoes in their worn out state, not even those drifters who grabbed everything as they walked through the neighborhood.

A stranger seated at a table in her bar was the first person beside herself to show any interest in the relics.

He had not said much since arriving, but his eyes were expressive as they focused on the leather ornaments at the toes of the shoes, as if he were trying to decipher an ancient code. Later, he explained that for a long time he had been looking for good trekking shoes to wear while travelling around the world. With her permission, he tried them on and made a few steps around the bar, but decided, somewhat baffled, that they were a bit tight.

It did not escape the other customers that he was treating these shoes as if they were somehow a lost treasure found at last. A few housewives sitting at another table were puzzled. Doesn't one take new shoes for a long journey, rather than worn-out boots that probably have passed more than a thousand miles?

He picked up one of the shoes, turned it upside down and shook it, then did the same with the other before returning both to the box. But he began to feel a kind of energy flowing from the shoes. The farmers asked him what he was doing. "Maybe if you wear them for a while they'll stretch out, or perhaps they're simply not your size and you need a different pair."

"These *should* be my size, but there's something stuck inside them, some kind of energy, making them tight," he insisted. "I wonder if these are the lost shoes, 'the magic pair'. Don't let appearances fool you. You won't find such quality at any fancy shoe store. Touching them, I can feel a sense of a long marvelous voyage, exactly what I was looking for."

The housewives at the near table looked at each other. "These are just simple shoes," said one of them. The barefoot stranger obviously had a serious issue with shoes.

He straightened his hat, which was a gift from a detective from another town, and murmured, "They could be angel's shoes."

"I have never heard of a firm called 'Angel Shoes'," one farmer said. "Is it famous?"

"These shoes belonged to an angel."

The farmer was not amused. "So how do you suppose they got here? Has an angel lost them during one of his flights?" he sneered.

Some faces around showed indifference, some curiosity. Complete surprise reigned at the housewives' table - no one was able to understand why this stranger treated these worn boots as mystical things. He picked up one shoe and brought it to his ear, while the housewives wondered if he were hearing an angels' song. As he laid it back down, the stranger's glance went beyond the pair of shoes, cutting across the street, between the walls of the houses. A half-mile further on, the bay seemed as it always had, with its same heavy blanket of fog. He caught a glimpse of a wing; a bird was circling the water silently, as if searching for drowned notes.

The landlady glanced thoughtfully at the stranger as she handed him another cup of tea. Guests with strange ideas were a part of the bar's tradition, but this guy broke all the records!

Taking a seep, he eased backward in his chair, beginning the story of the shoes - rumors pieced together. Some thought it sounded like Greek mythology; others felt it was other-worldly, but all listened intently.

Shoes were a motif in the first dream, the dream that started everything, a spark of the universal destiny. Before the world existed, shoes and stones swam randomly in space. Then the angels were put in charge of the design of

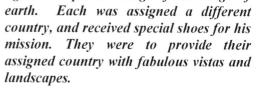

earth. Each was assigned a different country, and received special shoes for his mission. They were to provide their assigned country with fabulous vistas and landscapes.

One country remained empty, as its angel postponed his mission and instead travelled around the world to receive inspiration. When he tired and took some rest near the border of his country, he found a small shed. As he looked through the window, there was nothing but a thick fog from across the border.

He took off his shoes, put them on the windowsill and went to sleep. He noticed a bird playing with the shoelaces with its beak before flying away; one wing fading, the other rising, barely detectable in the mist. The blustery March wind was blowing.

No one knows exactly what happened that night. Some said that the shoes trembled and then a stream of sand along with hot ash flowed from within them for hours, days, or, maybe even more, spreading like lava from a volcano.

However, at sunrise, the angel woke up, and a fresh new landscape was revealed to him. His country was ready. He flew above, noticing the different variations from one end to another - seacoast, mountains, valleys, forests, deserts, and rivers rolling to the horizon. There were all kinds of views, and it seemed to him that a part of every country he had visited was represented here in his country, pieced together into a miniature of the entire world.

The work was done, but back in heaven, the angel realized that he had forgotten the shoes. After a while, he returned to search for them, but they were gone.

The drifter, who found the shoes in the shed on his way back home, put the shoes on the windowsill of his room before went to bed.

On morning, he noticed the view outside was different. There was no sign of the grassy terrains stretched out there; a hill rose instead, as if flushed out by the shoes. Afraid of their power, he hurried to get rid of those shoes throwing them as far as he could from home.

The shoes then passed from one person to another, as if on a journey of their own - thrown to the side of the road by one drifter, picked up by another traveler unable to afford new shoes of his own. Vagabonds repeated to each other how their travels with the shoes were easy, completely unlike journeys wearing any other shoes. They also said that the sun shone on the footprints left behind. The shoes were extremely flexible and fit every foot. They created a road, a road which fulfilled the destiny of every wearer. The last thing you want when you go on a journey is a dream to weigh you down. And these shoes made dreams come into existence.

The stranger took another seep from his tea.

It seemed that whenever someone put them on the windowsill of his room before going to bed, the usual view outside changed during the night, and he would wake up in a place he had never been. As if a stream flowing from the shoes, formed a new landscape which fit the traveler's dream, soul-made, sprawling, evolved. There were reports about new forests rising in the middle of deserts, hills and mountains appearing in oceans. All caused by the dreams of the travelers who found the magic shoes. **They make possible a real connection between the soul of whoever owns them and the ground;** *they show us the way.* **You can go with them to places never seen before,** *explore new dimensions.* **They make dreams come true. Angels need such shoes to connect to the earthy dimensions.**

The stranger ended and warned the farmers not to touch the shoes, as they were gifts from heaven. He added that even angels cannot escape normal procedures - when they come down to earth, they need shoes like everyone else. These shoes are a kind of gateway through which angels can fit into this world. Without them, angels would not have been able to come down to earth and shape the world, with all its views as we know them today. Without them, angels lose orientation on earth and feel as if they were stuck in a cave. They need these shoes to pave a route for them through the earth and then back to heaven. *They might not be effective anymore, but just in case.*"

The housewives were puzzled. "Everyone needs to believe in something," said one of them. "Some people carry mascots. For others, herbs can be more precious than jewels. Everybody wants tips and taps on the shoulder, anything that they think might help them."

"But shoes…?"

Angel's shoes or not, the bar owner was pleased by the streams of people from the city and the near villages coming into her bar in the next days; everyone was waiting to see what would come out of the magic shoes. Her bar, an inheritance from a distant relative, had never been so crowded. With each day, the usual quiet of the place, broken now and then by the presence of a few locals, was replaced by louder and louder roars of voices. Drifters with packs on their backs passed in the street, throwing envious glances at the windowsill, giving the bar much more attention than usual. More than to some toothbrushes that fell unnoticed from the kits of the fascinated drifters. Some of them hoped their dreams would come true any minute.

"These shoes probably need more time to demonstrate the efficiency of their workings," the housewives explained.

*

"If a local like me has trouble finding his way sometimes, then anybody would, even angels," a customer, who wore two different socks, observed on the next morning. "As a pilot in the army, I've got wings too - but even so, it's difficult. The question is, what are angels? I think they're entities with no physical body, which is why they need special shoes when they come down to earth."

A homemade yogurt with cherries lay on his table when the stranger arrived and sat down, and as he ate he picked on the housewives at the next table. He tried to explain the consequences of leaving the shoes on the windowsill. "These shoes have paved long paths, judging by how worn they are. They need more time - the dream stuck within them is a long one."

One farmer turned to him in a half-amused, half-serious tone, "Are you saying that some kind of lava is going to come out of one shoe, and create something according to the bar owner's dream?"

"This is how the shoes work. Dreams coming into existence from angel's shoes shatter the horizons of realities. They give free access to other dimensions. When humans finds them, anything may burst out, a whole stream. This was one condition: if the wearer picked up the shoes too soon from the window, and even one stone remained stuck inside, his whole journey would be uncomfortable, and the road not completed. The last stone is most valuable - not only does it mark the end of the road for the traveler…"

He did not finish the sentence, letting them figure out that the last stone must have a special quality, maybe even remarkable magical powers.

Out of curiosity, the bar owner examined the shoes again, and suddenly shook her head. "It's not a pair at all," she cried. "They're both left feet!"

The housewives chorused in derision, "No wonder one shoe is tight!"

Everyone in the bar looked at him with surprise. What can be expected of someone who wears two left shoes??

The stranger remained calm, throwing a glance at a clock on the wall. "The extra left shoe is because there's a dream stuck inside it. It's hard to say yet in which of the shoes, but it will turn into a right shoe as soon as everything gets out of it. These shoes should have worked by now…For some reason, the dream is still stuck; it must be a long one…"

The curious bar owner picked up one shoe, looking at it from all sides, but she had no desire to wear them. Lifting the shoe over her head, she noticed a tag on the bottom, "Made in Italy".

"I thought they were made in heaven," she smiled.

"Originally yes, *the sole and the inside of each shoe where made in heaven,* but some material was added in Italy later," he explained calmly. "Ever since, Italians are the world's best shoe designers."

He begged her to put it down, but she pointed to the wide mirror hung on the opposite wall. No reflection appeared there, as if the shoe didn't exist at all. She swung the shoe in all directions, but nothing happened. She was about to quit when the mirror creaked as if it were becoming heavier; a glimmer passed all over the wooden frame and a magnificent view was revealed. The bar owner thought she was daydreaming. The picture in the mirror seemed so real that one could walk straight into it.

He explained that the visions in the mirror were of Italy, the shoes' origin. His voice was low; when she laid the shoe back down, the views faded and only stars shone brightly all over the looking glass like dogs sniffing the corners of the universe.

He noticed the gray cat craning his neck from the nearby chair, as if he were an angel just awakened on a cloud, trying to obtain a better view. The stars soon faded, but the cat's tail kept wagging in superstitious alarm. The pet (the bar regulars called him Sal) seemed to miss his regular place in the window box, where he could see lovely sights, a fishing boat or a seagull leaving a white trail in the misty bay. He turned his gaze to a television screen hung over the bar. He was not a fan, except for the National Geographic channel and his favorite serial, 'CSI-Animals'; the main characters there, big cats looked wilder than in nature.

Suddenly, he jumped and tucked his head inside one shoe, his whine echoing an angel's song. He jumped backward to the chair, seemingly calmer, letting his gaze flutter over the customers like a disapproving fashion critic - nothing escaped him, from a farmer wearing two different socks to a homemaker with too-colorful lipstick.

Sal looked with the same precision at the reflection of two big eyes as the landlady glanced again at the mirror.

Later, the stranger asked her to call a carpenter, and an old man who had retired years ago, arrived, and started to pick out nails from a tool box and hammer them into the window box, "to strengthen and stabilize it as the burst of energy coming from the shoes might explode any moment," in the words of the stranger.

He urged the carpenter to work faster.

> *Destiny is a waiter. Past and future are served in dainty portions at the table.*

*

She was wearing a long gray dress, resting, when a glass of juice on the table moved a bit towards her. She looked at the carpenter in wonder, but he just shrugged, unable to give an explanation. Seemingly-bored he turned, his eyes twinkling; no wind blew through the window, not even the slightest breeze. Yet the shoelaces of one shoe swung in the air as if shaken by the wind, while the shoelaces of the other shoe were still.

A couple of farmers who were standing near the door turned around when they heard a noisy rustle; apparently it came from within the shoe. The cat jumped down from the chair he was hiding in, blinking about from beneath the near table.

The stranger scooped up the sleeves of his jacket; was it the moment he has been waiting for? At last, the dream-weavers, as some called these shoes, were functioning, demonstrating the efficiency of their working…

The noise became louder than rolling boulders. Then a stone shot out of the shoe with a whistle and flew across the street. Another stone flew away… A few more followed, shooting higher and higher, past the houses, half a mile farther, where they fell, swallowed by the coastal fog. All the people stood as still as astrologists watching a meteor shower.

Stones continued to come out, flung out from the shoe as if by an inner force, and flew into the dimness, as if each stone knew its own place. Stones in different sizes and shapes mixed with clods of sand and ash; the dream-stream increased its flow, as strong and smooth as a river. The coastal fog swirled over all. Blurred silhouettes cropped up with each passing moment. But after a period of time which could have been either years or only a few moments, the stream weakened, leaving just the memory. The shoe rested near its fellow, and as they looked at it, they saw that it had become a right shoe.

Silence reigned. Stunned farmers tried to understand what had just happened, but they could discern only clouds of dust still coming from inside the shoe.

Some noticed the barefoot stranger grabbing the shoes and disappearing quickly into the distance. They understood that he was fulfilling his dream of a long journey wearing the magic shoes. Only his hat was found later, rolling in the wind across the street, as if its owner had dropped off the face of the earth.

Everybody rushed outside, anxious to see how the coast had changed, and the bar owner soon followed, after searching the bar mirror. The cat was left looking at the fading reflection of her eyes, which were like leaves drifting slowly in the wind. When they were gone, he noticed his reflection in the mirror slowly changed into a bird. The bird in the mirror began to sing and flap its wings in time to the cat's blinks. He closed his eyes and heard the bird's wings flutter and fade into the distance, until the bird was just a small spot on the horizon, a white flash on the mirror.

He was free. He jumped to the windowsill. His gray and white fur became part of the coastal fog.

Turning his gaze to the bay, he saw two cliffs standing proudly, in huge proportion, rising from nowhere in the air.

They stood near the coastline and seemed to be moving, entangled by the coastal fog; their outlines the shape of shoes: two shoes, left and right, worn and wrinkled as if they had walked through a thousand memories, to the heart of the sea.

> *Stars are clues shining on the mystery of the universe.*

EPILOGUE

The crowd along the coastline varied hugely from scruffy students to suited business people escaping the city for an hour, and elderly pensioners walking along their dogs who chased a drifting newspaper or nylon bag. Some people said that they saw an angel perched on the top of one cliff, waving with his wings. The hiss of the waves crashing below and the flutter of his wings mingled into one swish as he dispersed into a misty wave. Fog is a heavy, living thing which dies slowly - no one knows what hides beneath it until it disappears. The bar owner just arrived, looking at the cliffs and wondering where the last stone had fallen. Wherever it was, according to the stranger, it should have shone brightly, brighter than any of the other stones. But only the person who found the shoes could see the glow – to other eyes, it remained a simple stone.

The stranger had also told her that the stone would fall at a particular spot, at the feet of the finder's soul-mate. He had explained to her that soul mates were two souls who had solved and completed one dream together.

It must have fallen farther, she thought to herself.

She kept going until she reached the town. Passing through one suburb after another, she began to wonder, *"The stranger was in a hurry to wear the shoes, but what if they weren't empty at all, and the last stone was still inside the shoe?"*

She walked toward the town center, a jam of trolleys, buses, and cars against the backdrop of huge buildings; and then stopped; a small park was revealed. The weather was fine, and a few people were sitting on the benches. She looked around searching for a free bench when something shiny caught her eye. The last stone lay within her reach.

*

It wasn't time for his lunch break yet. Some paperwork lay on his desk since morning, and he knew that his clients were waiting to hear about organized tours and vacations. But there was something peculiar in the air today and he had to go outside; the city looked different, as if shrouded by some kind of mist, a glamorous filter: everything seemed wonderful; tall buildings, cars, parades, and colorful billboards. And he remembered the dream he had that night. The memory flashed through his brain.

He sat on the bench and felt comfortable. Then a *sudden tap sounded, first one and then another. He turned and saw two worn high shoes that lay nearby on the bench, as if they had fallen from the sky, or were maybe flung from an airplane flying high above the city. But it was probably more sensible to think that they had been left by a drifter who had slept there that night. He picked them up. They fit…*

The travel finished his reverie, left his office and sat in the park, his gaze drifting to the building he had just left. He felt so much comfortable that he was wondering if it was a dream at all, or…

…Suddenly, a woman sat at the other side of the bench.

"What's so interesting in that building?" she asked him, bent forward and picked some stone that lay near his feet.

Soft dark ringlets obscured her face and her shoulders. When she turned, their eyes met and he discovered two large almond-shaped eyes. Like two leaves drifting in the wind, watching him - one of his eyes shone brightly. And nothing has ever felt truer or more precise and graceful. At that moment, his dream was solved.

A bird singing on the top of the tree spread its wings and flew away. Their gazes followed it and they saw the shoe-shaped cliffs rising as far and high as tall buildings of the outskirts.

When there is no solution to a dream, the one most improbable must be the truth, she said; it is not a dream at all but merely reality. Those shoes were lost by an angel.

The mist lifted over the cliffs, past the blue expanses of the sea, over green forests, and toward irregular mountains. On the horizon, a winding coastline was calling them.

The bird was a tiny spot in the distance. A blue sky emerged, with clouds drifting from afar. Clouds in the colors of the shoelaces, shaded violet and orange, passed over the mountains, plains and rivers. Somewhere, a wayfarer keeps the journey going. Every stone on the new route is a footprint of a dream.

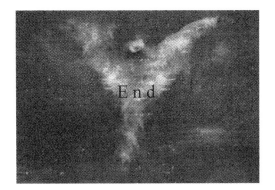

Dream Is The Verdict

The soul can walk a road that extends for miles

and miles but only if you stop for a while

can you enjoy the extent of the views.